PRAISE F~~OR~~ ~~.........~~ ~~......~~

"Thor, Baldacci, Flynn, Hamburg. Get ready as Banner fits right in!"

"Move over Jack Reacher there's a new guy taking over."

"Great stuff. Exciting and fast paced. On par with Flynn & Thor."

"The writing was superior, the story line was compelling and the action was top-notch. Sorry I could only give this one a five star rating!"

THE UNAVENGED

A HARRY BAUER THRILLER

BLAKE BANNER

RIGHTHOUSE

HARRY BAUER THRILLER SERIES

PROLOGUE

THEY CAME WITH THE COLD, GRAY DAWN. THEY CAME from the north on the Shali road, and from the east on the road from Avtury: two long columns moving slow and lazy through the dim light toward the town of Novye-Yurt.

As they arrived they slowed and fanned out with care and precision. The armored cars took up positions on the main streets, the Jeeps and Land Rovers in the smaller side streets. In the remaining alleyways, footpaths and side roads, foot soldiers took up their positions.

The townspeople peered at them from their windows, from their shops and from the early-morning cafés where the farmers and workmen were having breakfast.

At eight AM, Timur Edilov, the mayor, Salambek Zaytseva, his secretary, and Zaur Bazurkaev, the chief of police, approached the armored car on Ulitsa Kadyrova, the main street of the town. Unlike the armored cars on the other streets, this one was flanked by a Land Rover and a Jeep. The three men were surprised to discover, as they approached the vehicles, that the colonel standing in front of the armored car with his arms crossed over his chest, and the soldiers surrounding him, were not Russians. They were Chechens like themselves. The surprise was replaced by a sick, hollow feeling of helplessness and dread when they realized that this was Colonel Abbas Magomadov, and these were soldiers from the 141st Special Motorized Regiment, otherwise known as the Kadyrovitsy, the private army of the Kadyrov family, used amongst other things to do the dirty work not even the Russians would touch.

Mayor Timur Edilov tried hard, and failed, to keep the tremor from his voice.

"Colonel Magomadov, what is the meaning of this blockade? Why are your men and your tanks blocking the entrance and exit to the town?"

Magomadov was tall, lean and fair for a Chechen. He had always liked to believe that he was from Cossack descent. He held a cigarette in the fingers of his right hand. He examined the burning tip for a moment, spat elaborately at his feet and squinted through the smoke at the mayor as he took a deep drag.

"We have information, Mayor Edilov, that you harbor separatist rebels in this town."

"No!" The mayor shook his head violently, with terror hot in his chest. "No, we have never harbored rebels. We are just old men! Women! Young children and their mothers! Please, we have no rebels here! Have mercy! Have pity!"

"Pity? Mercy?" He looked at the men around him and they started to laugh. "What are you saying, Mayor Edilov? Are you accusing the Kadarovitsy of being criminals? That sounds to me like the seditious talk of a rebel."

The mayor's face seemed to fold in on itself and he began to sob. Zaur Bazurkaev, the chief of police, stood beside his friend. They were cousins, they had been to school together, played and fished in the river together as children. He appealed to the colonel, "I am the chief of police, Colonel. I can vouch for the mayor, he is a good and loyal man, we have never had rebels in this town. We are all loyal, please, we are a harmless village. Just women and children and a few old men..."

The colonel smiled as he sucked the last of the smoke from his cigarette and dropped it on the road. There he crushed it with his boot.

"Are you telling me, Sergeant, that a Chechen woman cannot fire a gun?"

Chief Bazurkaev spread his hands. "The women in this village..." He trailed off, raising his shoulders. "They cook, they clean, they look after their husbands and their children."

The colonel turned then to the secretary and jerked his chin at him. "And you, Mr. Secretary Zaytseva, what do you say? I have information from reliable sources that you are harboring criminals, traitors and rebels in this town. Do you think my informant is a liar, like these two?" He pointed at the mayor and the police chief.

The secretary shook his head. "I am sure your informant is not a liar, Colonel."

"He is telling the truth, then!"

"But equally, sir, I promise you that we have no rebels here. We are a simple town, we work, we obey... I don't know how your informant got his information—"

"What are you trying to do, Mr. Secretary Zaytseva?"

The secretary shook his head, not understanding the question. "Trying to do, sir...?"

"Are you trying to confuse me? Do you think I am stupid?" The colonel stared at the secretary. The morning was still, cold and silent. The mayor, the police chief and the secretary stared back at the colonel. Somewhere distant, among the trees, a bird chattered. The secretary said quietly, "No..."

The colonel turned to his captain and gestured at the secretary with his open hand. "Here is the evidence we needed. He is trying to confuse and bewilder me. My informant is not lying, he says, but there are no rebels here. Yet, clearly, if my informant is not lying, then there are rebels here!"

Again the secretary shook his head. "No..."

It was a denial, but more than that it was a plea for mercy. But Colonel Abbas Magomadov was not there to dispense mercy. He was there to bring death. He pulled his MP-443 Grach from its holster and shot the secretary in the head. The man swayed and folded to the ground. The mayor and the police chief began to sob, holding their hands out as though their fragile palms could ward off bullets. The colonel shot the mayor first, through his palm and between the eyes, and the police chief last, in the back, as he turned to run.

He lay groaning, coughing and dribbling blood from his perforated lungs. The colonel stepped up to him, placed his foot on the man's back and pressed. He took aim at the back of his head and fired once.

And that was the beginning. He climbed up into his Land Rover, picked up his radio and as it crackled in his hand he said, "OK! Advance, let's find these rebels!"

The advance was not rapid, it moved deliberately, in stages, house by house. The boots ran, tramping on the hardtop. Fists and boots hammered on doors, and soon the screaming started, women and crying children. But the weeping and the begging did not elicit compassion. When you put men into uniforms, they leave their humanity in the changing rooms. The weeping and the begging elicited shouts, aggressive and bullying as the soldiers invaded one home after another, dragging the families out into the streets, herding them and pushing them, with their hands held high, toward the town square.

Then there was a shot. It was a single, heartless, pitiless, irreversible crack. It had a small echo which trailed among the facades of the houses. It was followed by a cold stillness. A moment of abject terror, a shared moment of awful realization among the soldiers and the people they were going to kill. A line had been crossed, and now there was no way back. Then the killing started.

It started with the soldiers opening up on the gathered crowd. It didn't last long, twenty or thirty seconds of rattling and crackling; a lot of screams soon replaced by quiet sobbing, and sporadic single shots.

A moment of silence followed as the soldiers looked down on

what they had done. It was broken by the bellowing voice of an officer, and the soldiers launched into a rampage, driven by some half-articulated sense that if they did not stop, if they sank deeper into the carnage and pitiless madness, somehow guilt and remorse would be crushed, smothered, drowned in blood. So that the terrified eyes of the children and the aged, and the twisted, heart-broken faces of the wailing mothers and fathers would cease to have meaning, cease to torture their minds and hearts.

Minds and hearts that in most cases had been those of school-children barely two or three years earlier.

They ran, swarming over the gates and walls, ever present in Chechen villages and towns, shooting out locks, kicking in doors and smashing windows, not bothering now to drag people out of their houses, but shooting them where they found them. Those who managed to flee from their houses were shot down in the roads by the armored cars.

Not all the females were killed. The younger ones, some as young as eleven and twelve, were raped or taken as sex slaves to be gifted to the commanders. By eleven o'clock that morning, Colonel Magomadov had accumulated six young girls to serve him.

The massacre did not end that day, nor did the pillaging. It continued for a week longer. The colonel set up a base in the town, effectively turning it into a concentration camp, and the inhumanity continued at a leisurely pace for the next six days. Public executions were preceded by public mass rapes and followed by sessions of public torture whose purported purpose was to obtain information about the whereabouts of the men of the town, but whose real purpose was to instil terror and bring the population of Chechnya as a whole into submission. There was no information, no answer those interrogated could have given, that would have changed their fate.

After a week the population of Novye-Yurt, which had stood at slightly less than ten thousand inhabitants, had been reduced to slightly less more than six hundred girls between the ages of eleven and twenty-two. Some would be given to commanders and officials, others they would sell into Europe, America and the Middle East, through Poland.

On the seventh day Colonel Magomadov ordered the retreat from the town. The columns left as they had come, with the cold, gray dawn, into the north along the Shali road, and into the east along the road to Avtury: two long columns moving slow and lazy through the dim light toward the next village reported to harbor anti-Russian rebels.

However, by the time his column had reached Agishty, just three and a half miles south of Novye-Yurt, Colonel Magomadov had called a halt. He instructed his second in command, Captain Vakha Umarov, to camp outside the town and leave the townsfolk in peace. He took a Jeep and drove back, retracing his steps from the town, but he did not stop when he got there. Instead, he continued on, climbing ever higher into the forests among the peaks of the Caucasus Mountains.

Much later his Jeep was found abandoned among the trees outside Agavi, just a few miles from the border with Georgia and the wilderness of the Tusheti National Park. There was no sign of the colonel. Nobody had seen him, there was no blood, no sign of a firefight, no sign of struggle. He had simply vanished without a trace.

There were those who knew him who said that he had been ambushed and killed by Chechen separatist rebels. Others said that the weight of the atrocities of the Kadarovitsy had become too much for him and he had become a hermit in a cave on the border. Still others said he had been abducted by aliens who had punished him for his cruelty by sending him to a galactic prison camp on Ganymede. A very few, a small handful, said he feared Russia could not guarantee him safety from prosecution by the International Court of Human Rights, and he had run and changed his identity, taking stolen loot with him, to the one place in the world he believed nobody would ever look for him.

That had been just after the turn of the millennium.

ONE

I was in Bolinas Altas looking for Abe McGore because the brigadier and the colonel had identified him as Colonel Abbas Magomadov, who had led the massacre of three towns in Chechnya at the turn of the millennium, and then disappeared with twenty million bucks' worth of stolen art treasures and cash. Over the years various agencies had tried to track him down in Chile, Brazil, Mexico and Colombia, with not much success. Africa and the Indian Ocean had proved equally unfruitful, and finally the trail had gone cold. Until 2020, when an anonymous tip-off had placed him in Northern California.

Then a little known agency attached to the Five Eyes treaty, that went by various misleading names, had found a trail that went from Chechnya through Georgia to Turkey and then went cold. It went cold until a guy in the Passport Office in Ankara, who could arrange you a genuine Turkish passport for a fee, even if you weren't entitled to it, was persuaded to remember that in 2005 he had issued a special, green passport to a man who might have been Chechen. It had been issued in the very un-Turkish name of Abraham Major, as the man claimed to be naturalized Turkish of British origin.

That trail had eventually led the operative from the so-called

Office of the Democratic Intelligence Network, based in Arlington, Virginia, to New Zealand. From New Zealand he had moved on to Australia, and there his trail had gone cold again. Until the operative, who clearly knew how to do his homework, found Abraham Major's death certificate. The British-born naturalized Turk had, apparently, died while exploring the Australian outback. Most of him had been consumed by various inhabitants of the wilderness, but his right hand and one leg, and his rucksack, had been found intact. The rucksack contained his papers and ID, and that had apparently been enough to ID him.

But the operative, not one to be easily satisfied, had dug deeper, and a search through passports granted in the two months following the discovery of Abraham Major's body had thrown up one Abe McGore, who had requested an Australian passport and, shortly afterwards, a United States visa. This had in turn yielded a passport photograph, a request for a resident's permit and a work permit in California; and finally a Social Security Number.

A few final checks, including the use of facial recognition software, had made it incontrovertible. Abe McGore, the guy living at 17 Manzanilla Avenue in Bolinas Altas, overlooking the Bolinas Altas golf course and the Gulf of the Farallones, just twenty miles north of San Francisco as the crow flies was, beyond any kind of doubt, Abbas Magomadov.

He was apparently a man of private means who lived off the interest from foreign investments; probably trusts set up in British dependencies nurtured by the City of London. According to his file, part of his money he had invested in some kind of quasi-religious cult with a charitable status. Whether he had set it up himself or simply bought into it was not clear. Neither did it really matter. I wasn't there to write his biography. I was there to kill him.

Bolinas Altas was a leafy, residential area where people who could afford it came to retire and play golf, or families who could afford it came to protect their kids from the modern world they had conspired to create. From there they commuted to the hive for work every day, to help consolidate the world they wanted to protect their kids from. It was quiet. Every house had its plot of land with a pool and gardens, a high wall and a big gate. Each cell was almost identical to the next.

Manzanilla Avenue was situated high up, near the heart of Bolinas Altas Village, near Main Street and the Farmers' Market. From there it curled down in a big sweep, past the golf course, toward the coast and Palomarin Beach.

Magomadov's place was a two-story villa with a swimming pool. It was set among palm trees, and had a Spanish-style orange-tiled roof which was turning pink in the dying sun. There was an iron gate with a wooden name plate beside it that read "Eden." The gate was open and there was nothing telling me to beware of the dog. So I stepped through, closed the gate behind me and climbed the steps through the exotic garden to the front door.

It was a sultry evening. The heat hung humid in the still air, though the light was turning a grainy blue-gray, with a few pastel pink tinges only nature could get away with. I could make out the smell of barbequing meat from neighboring gardens, and some-where people were laughing. You could almost hear the tinkle of ice in their tall glasses, and see the warm glow spilling from their French windows onto their patios.

Only there was no light spilling from Magomadov's front door or windows, and the only sounds were the lapping of the water in his swimming pool and the high-pitched grinding of the *cicadas* on the warm air. I rang the bell and hammered on the door, but there was no reply. So I took a walk round back and explored his shrubs and flower beds, his patio and the French doors. Then I stood a moment staring into his pool, thinking about the fact that, like his gate, the French doors onto the patio were not quite closed. They had been left half an inch open. Whoever had left the gate open had pulled the French doors too, without closing them.

Finally I went, slid them opened and stepped inside. It was dark, silent and oppressively warm. I didn't put the lights on. I waited for my eyes to adjust and then had a look around. I was in a big dining-room-cum-sitting-room affair which extended into an open-plan kitchen. There was no one there and everything looked clean, tidy and well ordered. There were no family pictures and no photo albums.

Over on the right there was a staircase that ascended to the top floor. I climbed it. The stairs creaked, but the creaks got no response. No voices called to see who I was.

I got to the landing and stopped. It was darker upstairs and I had a prickling feeling in the back of my neck. There was a banister on my left overlooking the stairs, and on my right I could make out two doors, with a third right ahead of me. The two on my right were closed, but the one ahead of me was open.

Dark blue moonlight reflected off the ocean gave the room an eerie luminescence. I could see plate-glass doors that stood open, and the moonlight was making silhouettes out of a balustrade, a round table and a chair.

And an unsettling pile on the floor.

I walked quietly into the room and stood in the doorway. I could now see the moon setting over the Pacific far below. I looked at the dim stars in the turquoise sky, I looked at the swaying palms, and finally I forced myself to look down at the mess, the remains of the man lying in the pool of blood; blood which outrageously reflected the peaceful light of the moon.

He had been dismembered. His legs lay at grotesque angles to his body. His left arm lay with the hand pointing to his hip and the shoulder toward the balustrade. His right hand was by his feet and his head, on the table, sat grinning savagely out at the sparkling, silver path the moon had laid across the black depth of the ocean. His thin, sandy hair moved in the evening breeze.

I pulled my cell from my pocket, took a short video of the scene and then photographs of the dead man's face from several angles. I sent them to the brigadier with a short message:

"Looks like somebody got here before me. Is this our guy?"

Then I stepped back into the dark house and took my

pencil torch from my inside pocket. I played the beam around the room and found it was some kind of an office or study. There was a computer on the desk to my left, and there were low bookcases against all the walls. To my right there were a couple of filing cabinets, a small sofa and a lamp on a small, heavy, marble-topped table. Some other time I might have nosed around some more to find out what he was about. Maybe I should have done that, but with a dismembered body lying out on the balcony I didn't feel like hanging around all that much. All I wanted was some clue as to who had beat me to the punch.

I sat behind his desk and pulled open the drawers, and let the circle of torchlight rest on the contents. There was nothing there but paper and ink, a stapler and some boxes of staples. There was also a passport in the name of Abe McGore. I picked it up and opened it. The picture looked like the head on the table. The few stamps there were seemed to be entering and leaving Mexico. No surprises there. I stood up and crossed the room to the filing cabinets. They weren't locked so I was pretty sure what I was going to find—nothing much.

I was wrong. The drawers were full of files, and each file was about a person. A quick flick through showed that these people had practically nothing in common. They were of all ages, from young children to people in their eighties; and they were of extremely varied backgrounds: from builders and tradesmen to academics, businessmen and women and professionals. In fact the only thing I could find that they shared in common was that they all belonged to his cult, the United Church of Nergal.

I went down to the kitchen, found a couple of plastic refuse sacks, returned to the terrace and collected his right hand. I also took one of the files. I used a cloth to remove my prints from anything I had touched and made my way back down the stairs and out into the balmy evening. The pool was still lapping and you could still hear the laughter and the music from the nearby barbeque. A chorus of frogs had added their voices to the revelries, but managed somehow to make it all sound peaceful and still under the moon.

I made my way out to the street and climbed into my rental car. The slam of the door insulated me inside the cab and I called the brigadier. As usual he made it sound like I was calling about an invitation to a cocktail party.

"Harry, good to hear from you."

"You got my pictures and the video?"

"Indeed. Very interesting. Any ideas?"

"No, but I think we need to get somebody in there before the cops or the Feds find him."

"Really? Why's that?"

"Call it a hunch, but I found a couple of filing cabinets full of files. There must have been a couple of thousand at least, on members of that cult he was involved with, the Church of..."

"The United Church of Nergal—"

"That one. I couldn't put it into words right now, but I know those files, and the state his body was in, add up to something that ain't mom's apple pie. Aside from anything else, I'd like to know how it was done. There was a hell of a lot of blood, which suggests it was done while he was alive, or in the process of dying. I didn't have time to inspect the wounds, but I'd like to know if his limbs were hacked, sliced or surgically removed."

"I'm inclined to agree. I'll call the Director of Intelligence. They've had the case since Georgia. Did you recover anything?"

"Yeah..." I looked down the empty street, dimly lit by replicas of nineteenth-century gas lamps, and glanced in the mirror. There was nothing there but more empty street and more gas lamps. "I thought it was the Office of the Democratic Intelligence Network."

"Yes, well, as the Bard said, what's in a name? They're attached to the Five Eyes, as are we, so we cooperate."

"Right. In other news, I have a couple of presents for our forensic team."

"I thought you might. Is it his right hand?"

"Yes, sir, and a sample of the files."

"Good, Harry. Good work. I'll have someone collect them. Meanwhile, the job seems to have been done for us. So book yourself into a hotel in San Francisco and I'll be in touch in the next few hours."

I hung up and cruised down the Shoreline Highway, watching the smirking moon sink ever lower toward the horizon. At Manzanita I joined Highway 101 and let it carry me through the majestic trees that fringe the recreation area, and across the Golden Gate to the Presidio. There I called the Four Seasons and booked a room.

There was something playing on my mind as I cruised down Van Ness and turned into California Street at Nob Hill. I kept going over the dark living room, the dining room and the kitchen, the creaking stairs and the tidy, well-ordered den. I couldn't see anything in my mind, but my gut told me it was there; not upstairs, but somewhere between the living room and the kitchen.

Something that was wrong.

I could smell it. The voice in my head repeated it a couple of times, and I realized there had been a smell. I turned into Sansome Street, parked illegally outside the hotel, checked in and handed my keys to the valet parking valet along with twenty bucks. In the elevator I called Cobra and left a message for the brigadier, telling him where I was.

I had a long, hot shower, fantasizing that the scalding, soapy water could seep into my brain and wash away what I had seen.

When I climbed out of the shower my cell was ringing. I answered it with wet hands and water running down my face from my hair.

"Yeah."

"Harry, it's me, Jane..."

I went very still, ignoring the slow burn in my gut. "Hi, I was expecting the brigadier."

"Yes, I told him I'd call. I hope that's OK." She didn't sound ironic or sarcastic. "After..." She paused. "After Cabinda, we seemed to lose touch."

"That probably had something to do with my terrible timing. Every time I called you, you were out."

"I'm sorry about that, Harry."

"And when we did meet it was either in a briefing or a debriefing, and you always had to run afterwards."

"I'm sorry."

I shrugged. She couldn't see me, so I guess the gesture was for myself. "It's work. It's the way it goes. So who's coming for the package?"

"Don't be like that, Harry. I have apologized twice."

I took a deep breath and trailed water to the window overlooking the sparkling city. "I don't know what to say. Hell, I don't even know what to call you. It's always a helter-skelter ride with you. I never know from one turn to the next what to expect. One minute it's Marilyn Monroe, the next it's the girl next door and then it's the ice queen in a US Air Force uniform."

"That's unkind, but I guess I deserve it."

Her voice, the tone of her voice, made me soften and I couldn't stop a smile from entering mine. "I had my leg bitten off by a crocodile while rescuing you. Did you know that?"[1]

"Yes, I know, Harry. It didn't actually bite it off..."

"It almost bit it off. A couple of inches higher and it could have been serious. Not a lot of guys would do that for a girl."

"Can you forgive me, or do I have to keep apologizing?"

"I shouldn't. But yeah, I guess I have to."

"I heard you met somebody. A doctor, in Wyoming."

I floundered a moment. "Yeah, I...we...yeah..."

"Buddy says you're thinking of resigning, and setting up a ranch out there."

"The brigadier has a big mouth."

---

1. See *A Simple Kill*

"I almost hope you do, Harry; resign, I mean. Is she good for you?"

"I—I don't, I'm not ready for this—I'm not sure I'm ready for this conversation."

I heard her sigh at the other end of the line. "I hope she can help you escape from Al-Landy, from all the daemons."[2]

"Yeah, well, I don't see it that way, Jane. Because the other possibility, the more likely possibility, is that I'll drag her down into hell with me. That's why guys like me live alone. Because women who are foolish enough to get involved end up getting burned, and the smart ones steer clear and don't answer their phones."

She took so long to answer I began to wonder if she'd hung up. Finally she said, "That's not what happened. This isn't the time or the place—"

"No, with you it never is, Jane."

"This job looks like it's done. I seem to recall we have an appointment in New York that's well overdue. Maybe, when you return home..."

She trailed off, leaving her meaning hanging in the air.

"Sure, but when I get there, are you going to disappear again, and hide behind the brigadier and the job?"

"No. I'm here in San Francisco. I am going to collect the package from you in half an hour. When the job is done, we'll meet in New York, I promise."

"That's two promises you owe me."

There was a long silence. Then, "I know, Harry. I haven't forgotten."

---

2. See *The Dead of Night*

TWO

I WENT DOWN TO THE BAR AND ORDERED A DRY martini, then sat in the corner for half an hour with my cell, reading about the United Church of Nergal. That is, I started reading about the cult, and ended up getting distracted by Nergal. He was apparently a Sumerian god of war, death and disease who was described by Professor Frans Wiggerman of the Vrije University of Amsterdam as "the God of Inflicted Death."

Nergal was, according to the text I was reading, associated with the "Enki-Ninki" gods. That made me smile, but by all accounts Enki-Ninki gods were not small cute gods your kids could play with (as opposed to mighty gods of fire and brimstone). They were the ancestors of Enlil, another Sumerian god, and were believed to reside in the underworld. According to an ancient Mesopotamian hymn, dominion over the land of the dead was bestowed upon Nergal by his parents, Enlil and Ninlil (not to be confused with Enki and Ninki), and Nergal was believed to decide the fate of the dead.

In addition to being a god of the underworld, Nergal was also, perhaps appropriately, a god of war. He was believed to accompany kings and emperors into battle, and in peace to act as a deterrent, shades of Roosevelt and his big stick. Like Aries in Ancient

Greece, he was associated with the planet Mars. He carried a dagger, a bow and a mace, and a sword decorated with lions' heads.

There was more, mainly about his parents and other Sumerian gods called the Anunnaki, who for some reason I associated with UFOs and conspiracy theorists. But apparently, they were just ancient Sumerian gods, like Nergal—"the descendants of Anu" or "those who came from the sky." The article also stressed that Nergal had endured from the earliest times in Mesopotamia, right up to neo-Babylonian times.

I finished the article, sighed at the ceiling and sipped my martini. I figured that it made sense, if Abe McGore was Colonel Abbas Magomadov. If a guy who indulged in massacres was going to get involved with a cult, it would be a cult that glorified war and death. It probably also made sense that, instead of Mars or Aries or Odin, it would be something obscure like an ancient Sumerian god. But my mind went back to the filing cabinets full of files on members of the church, and for some reason I just couldn't put into words, it jarred. Something was wrong that wasn't right. I half smiled at my drink. I could just hear a thundering, mighty voice ringing out, "Beware ye puny mortals! For Nergal, God of War and Pestilence is wont to put ye...in his filing cabinet...?"

I had a look at the website for the United Church of Nergal. There was a lot of stuff about dying in life to become a mightier self, knowing your darkness in order to release your light, and how in ancient Sumeria there was not one, universal god. The gods were not gods as we think of them. They were the "Mighty Ones," and taught humans to develop their latent potential. Most of us, it said, had lost our lives—like you might lose your keys or your wallet—and as a consequence we lived in servitude. Nergal was the god of the underworld because he led those who had lost their lives to true, godly empowerment.

It ended with an invitation: if you wanted to unleash your own, mighty, godly potential, you had to call a San Francisco number or send an e-mail. All that was missing was the tagline, "It's never been so easy to become a god!"

I laid down my cell, telling myself that with a little luck the brigadier would decide our job had been done for us, and the task of investigating who had executed Colonel Abbas Magomadov would fall to the Office of Diabolically Intelligent Nerds, or whatever their name was.

I was having fun with my fourth version of the acronym ODIN (the Organization of Denuded Intellectual Nymphomaniacs) when Colonel Jane Harris, JSOC, walked into the bar. She stood a moment scanning the room, then spotted me and came over to my table. As she approached I stood, smiled and held out my hand.

"Colonel, it's good to see you."

She glanced at my hand, then looked me in the eye. "Harry, stop being an asshole."

I nodded a couple of times and couldn't help smiling and giving my head a twitch.

"It's not easy."

She sat. "It seems to me you have made a successful career out of doing things that are not easy. Now for Christ's sake stop feeling hard done by and give me a little latitude."

"When you put it like that."

"We need to set our personal issues to one side until this job is done. That doesn't mean we have to be hostile. And I'd like you to stop guilt tripping me."

I leaned back in my chair and signaled the waiter. Then I smiled at her. "Anything else?"

"That's not enough?"

"It's plenty."

"Then yes, what did you recover from the house?"

"A right hand and a file."

"Where are they?"

"The hand is in the fridge in my minibar. The file is in my safe. Have you run the photos I sent through facial?"

She nodded. "It's almost certainly him."

I gave her a smug smile. "One thing this Bronx punk learned from the brigadier—"

"What's that?"

"You can't qualify an absolute. Almost certain is not certain. It's either certain or it ain't."

"All right, Mr. Bronx Punk, it has a very high probability of being him. DNA from the hand will be conclusive."

"When will we know?"

"Early hours of the morning. Gin and tonic, please. Beefeater."

The last bit was directed at the waiter who had drifted up. He nodded and went away. I said, "So, if it's confirmed, I can go back to New York?"

She nodded a few times, watching my face and blinking. Finally she said, "Will you go to New York, or Pinedale?"

I couldn't look at her. I let my eyes trail across the illuminated bottles behind the bar, like I was interested in them; like I was looking for a particular gin or whiskey. In my mind's eye I could see Magomadov's dismembered body on the terrace, his nightmarish head grimacing out at the ocean and the moon, with the breeze moving wisps of hair on his forehead. I wanted to say that I was tired, tired of cruelty and killing, that I needed to find some peace and sanity. Instead I shook my head and said, "I can't think about that right now. Let's confirm that this was Magomadov, that the job is done. I'll go back to New York. Let's meet and talk, if you want to."

"I want to."

I nodded. "OK."

We sat while she drank her gin and tonic and discussed work, with patches of awkward silence scattered here and there. Finally we went up to my room and I gave her the gruesome parcel and the file, which she placed in an attaché case.

She paused at the door on her way out and told me, "I'll be in touch."

I didn't answer and she left the room and closed the door behind her, leaving a backwash of silence in her wake.

———

I DIDN'T HEAR anything that night, or in the small hours, from the colonel or from the brigadier. So the next morning, after breakfast, I took a ride to the Mission District.

The United Church of Nergal was on the corner of Guerrero and 23rd Street, in what had once been St James' Catholic Church. Its entrance was on Guerrero, and, appropriately, guerrero, in Spanish, means warrior. So either it had been a deliberate choice, or synchronicity had been at work. No doubt the faithful believed it was the hand of Nergal.

I parked my rental out front and stood a moment looking at the three great whitewashed arches. Five granite steps ascended to them. And once you had ascended, three iron gates topped with spikes forbade you access. It seemed that, though God was everywhere, if you wanted to see him or talk to him, you had to make an appointment.

I looked for a bell but didn't find one, so I took a stroll down 23rd. There I found an alley which was just called Ames, and another door set in a large arch. This one had been painted sage green and had a bell at the side. I leaned on the bell for five seconds and heard it jangle and echo inside.

Nothing much happened after that so I did it again. The flaw with Einstein's definition of insanity is that sometimes you have to do something more than once to get any result at all.

My third attempt, which went on for fifteen seconds, brought the echoing of footsteps, the rattle of a lock and the creaking of a door as it opened inward. The face that looked up at me belonged to a woman. It had everything you would need for extreme beauty, except warmth. It was a pale face that looked as if all the muscles in it had gone rigid through sheer outrage. She looked like an Aryan Presbyterian who'd just been reminded Jesus was a rabbi. She didn't say anything. Her face said it all for her: what the hell did I want? I smiled.

"Good morning. Is this the United Church of Nergal?"

Her eyes traveled down to my shoes, then took their time traveling up to my face again.

"Yes."

"I was reading about you on your website, and I have to say I was fascinated. I would be interested in making a contribution, and perhaps joining the church."

She didn't do anything. She just stood and stared at me and looked severe. When it started to become embarrassing I said, "Is there somebody I could talk to about membership, and a donation?"

Her eyes took another trip to my shoes and back again, after which she stepped back and pulled the door open wide.

"Come in."

I crossed the threshold into a small, dark hall with a domed ceiling and gray walls. Her perfume was strong on the air and had hints of jasmine and orange blossom. It was strangely at odds with her face and her expression.

On my right there was a heavy wooden door set in a gabled arch. She opened it and I followed her into the transept of the church. What light there was came from stained-glass windows set high in the walls of the nave. The echo of the door closing behind me seemed to roll up those walls among the heavy wooden rafters.

The floor was stone and completely exposed. All the benches had been removed, leaving a vast, empty space. Before I had a chance to get a good look she brushed past me and walked toward where I figured the altar must be, just out of sight.

Her steps ricocheted off the walls and rose to join the slammed door up in the shadows beneath the ceiling. I followed her, but before we got to the altar she turned left toward what had once been the vestry. She pushed through that door into what was now the admin office. There was a cluttered desk facing the door, and over on my right there was another desk with a computer.

Sitting at that desk was a man in his thirties with very short hair. He was typing and ignored me.

She sat and used her eyes to point at the chair across the desk. I obeyed and sat too.

"Who are you?" There was the slightest trace of an accent.

"Harry," I said. "Harry Bauer."

"Why are you interested in our church?"

I frowned and leaned forward. Her eyes narrowed. I said, "I am interested in death. I..." I hesitated, shifted my eyes to look at the wall, then brought them back to examine her face. It really was a beautiful, unlovely face. "I was in the British army. In special operations. I saw a lot of death. I killed a lot of men, lost friends. And I always wondered—maybe you'll think I'm crazy—I always wondered if there was another way to die. Do you have to lose your life when you die?"

The guy at the computer turned to look at me. He glanced at the woman, then turned back and kept typing. I waited for her to say something, but she obviously wasn't going to. So I went on.

"I've read a few books, I surf the Net, but I have never found anything that I felt could answer that question. Then last night I found your site, and I got the feeling maybe..." I shrugged and trailed off.

"Who do you work for?"

I let my eyebrows show I was surprised by the question.

"I don't work for anybody." I gave an embarrassed laugh. "I don't work. I, um... I have private means." She arched an eyebrow. I explained. "When I left the army I was able to use the skills I had learned in various ways: international transport in risky situations, assisting some third-world governments in various ways. It's work that pays well and affords opportunities for private enterprise." I winced. "Do I need to explain?"

"No. You were a mercenary and a gun runner."

"Thank you."

"There is no sin. There is no sin because there is no good. You understand?"

I frowned, like I was trying to understand. "I think so."

Her face made severity into a savage thing. "I am telling you, you cannot come here for forgiveness. There is no forgiveness, here or anywhere. If you are looking for compassion, empathy, redemption, fuck off and go to the Christians or the fucking Buddhists!"

I stared at her for a long moment, fascinated in spite of myself. She went on. "If there is no right or wrong, then there is no forgiveness." She raised her finger and shook it in the negative. "If you are looking for forgiveness, you will not find it here. If you are looking for a mighty god who can reach down and wash away your sins, you will not find him here. Do you understand this?"

"Yes."

"In the Church of Nergal we seek death. We die, and in dying we open our eyes to the truth. We see the lies, we see the fog of dreams, we see the walls and barriers of beliefs, and we watch them all fall away, and decay. And then we step into life, free."

"I want that," I said, and almost meant it. "I need that."

"How much can you pay?"

The question caught me by surprise. I faltered a moment. "I don't know... Is that what this is about, money?"

"*Wake up, Harry!* Money, power, what else? We can make you free, but you fucking pay! How much can you pay?"

I flopped back in my chair, trying to think fast. "Uh, I'd need to check my accounts. A thousand bucks?"

"Get out."

"No, wait, hang on, five—five thousand bucks!"

Her face flushed red. "*Get out!*"

I raised both hands. "Stop it, will you! Let me think!"

She leaned forward, her face still flushed, shouting at me across the desk. "*You got rich smuggling guns and killing people! You talk bullshit about needing freedom! But you can't afford more than five thousand dollars? You are full of shit, Harry!*"

"*All right!*" I leaned forward and roared into her face. "*One hundred thousand dollars!*"

There was total silence in the room. The guy had stopped typing and was staring at his screen. The color subsided from her face. She smiled.

"Can you do it?"

"Yes, but I can't go down to the ATM and get it. I'll have to make arrangements."

She leaned back in her chair. She was still smiling. There was something like warmth in her eyes. But it wasn't warmth as we know it, Jim.

"What kind of arrangements?"

"You have an offshore account?"

She nodded. "More than one."

"Then I'll talk to my accountant about a transfer. Give me what I want and it might be the first of several."

"Welcome to the United Church of Nergal, Harry."

THREE

I RESPONDED TO HER SUB-ZERO SMILE WITH A SMILE OF my own, which I tried to lace with predatory menace. It wasn't hard. She evoked that kind of feeling in a man. She evoked it in me, anyway.

"Show me the church, and explain to me how this works. You know enough to do that?"

"I know enough to do that."

She stood and left the room, leaving the door open behind her. I followed her back into the nave. She walked quickly to the middle of the huge, stone-flagged floor and turned to face me. She looked small and indistinct among shadows. Her voice, when she spoke, was harsh.

"Nergal is one of the most ancient gods on the planet. He came in the beginning, when the sky was first split from the Earth, and life was separated from death." Her rhythm said she was reciting, but there was passion in her voice, like she believed what she was saying, and it was doing something for her. "An created duality. Utu became the god of the sun, Ninhursag, the Mother and the mountain, the goddess of fertility. Inanna was the goddess of love, war, fertility, sex and political power. And Nergal the god of death. But the Master tells us that, of all the Anunnaki, Nergal alone was the most important. Because all the other gods created dreams that were prisons for the faithful. But Nergal offered freedom through death."

I approached her and noticed as I drew close that eleven five-foot silver candelabra had been placed in a circle around where she stood, holding large, fat church candles. But directly in front of her, at the entrance to what had been the altar, stood a grotesque statue of some kind of humanoid. It seemed to be carved out of ebony, or some deep, black substance. It stood about eight feet tall, with small horns protruding from curly hair, fangs emerged from a half-open mouth and rested on a long beard.

In his right hand he held an axe and his left hand rested upon the hilt of a long sword that hung at his side. From his waist a rope descended to the necks of two brutish hounds, one of which was white. By his right side there was a tall staff, at the top of which two bull's horns formed a crescent moon resting on a bull's head. Beneath that was something that might have been an elongated egg, but a closer look revealed that it was an eye, with stylized eyelids and a pupil.

Beneath that were four disks, like large washers. The first of these was raised up, the lower three were folded down. On his chest he had, in relief, the image of a scorpion and a snake, and beside them the same images were sunk into the wood.

I said, "Is that Nergal?"

"No." Something about the way she said it made me look at her face. "That is a representation of Nergal." She took a step toward me. "A map can assist you to traverse a territory, but only a fool comes to believe that the map *is* the territory. That is not a god. That is a lump of wood that was carved by a person. To encounter the god, first you must die."

Behind the lump of wood there was a black marble altar standing under the high, vaulted ceiling of the apse. The crucifixes and any decoration or statues of saints that you might have found in the Catholic church had been removed. The walls had been painted a very dark blue, and the dome above was supported on bare wooden beams.

"What happens back there?"

She took another step and stood next to me. "There are rituals. You will learn them in time, as you progress."

I looked into her eyes; they were amused. "Progress?"

"Toward your death."

"What's your name?"

"You can call me Anna."

"Who founded this church, Anna?"

"You have so many questions."

"Is that a problem?"

"Only for you. It was founded by Abraham. He had suffered so long in hell, and one day he knew he could suffer no more, and so he ran into the mountains. And in the mountains, in the cold and the snow, he died and was reborn. In the moment of his rebirth he was faced with a choice. Should he keep the secret of death and rebirth to himself, or should he share it and teach it and help humanity to become free? He chose the second. Because he had caused a lot of suffering and pain in his life, and now he wanted to bring joy."

"He sounds like a soldier. Were the mountains in Afghanistan?"

It was the question a British or American special ops soldier might ask. I knew he hadn't been in Afghanistan, but I was curious to see if she would correct me. She did.

"The Caucasus. Abraham is a Chechen. But it is better if you hear his story from him directly."

"I'd like that. How does this work? Do you have regular meetings? Is there a particular day of the week...?"

"No." She shook her head. "We will be in touch. Your donation is very generous. When you make it, I am sure Abraham will want to meet you and thank you."

The hint was clear. I smiled and gave a single nod. "I'll talk to my accountant this afternoon. I'll call you..." I paused and held her eye. "Have you got a personal number I can call?"

"You want to have sex with me?"

"Well, I'm not in a desperate hurry. Maybe we could have dinner first."

She reached in the back pocket of her jeans and pulled out a wallet. From that she extracted a card and handed it to me. It told me she was Anna Molyboha, secretary of the United Church of Nergal. A cell number, but no address.

"Can I look Abraham up on Google? I like to do research."

She sniggered, only it was almost a sneer. "Filling in the details of your map?"

"I guess so."

"You can look him up. You won't find very much. Abe McGore."

"He anglicized his name?" She didn't answer. She studied my face. I sighed. "C'mon! I'm about to give the guy a hundred grand. I'd like to know a little about him."

"Yes, he anglicized his name. Before he was Abbas."

"Abbas?" I frowned hard, then turned narrowed eyes on her. "*Abbas? Abbas Magomadov?*"

I knew I had overplayed my hand, but you needed a crowbar to get anything out of this dame. She arched an eyebrow at me and I guess she was thinking of the hundred grand because she didn't kick me out. She said, "What do you know about Abbas Magomadov?"

"I told you, I was in British special ops. I joined about fifteen years ago and there was a lot of talk still about Abbas Magomadov and how he had disappeared after massacring a town in Chechnya."

"The town was Novye-Yurt."

I looked around and gestured at the church as a whole. "So this is him? This is Abbas *Magomadov*? He is wanted for war crimes and crimes against humanity."

She didn't answer for a while. She just watched me. Eventually she asked me, "So what are you going to do, continue to play in the dream, or follow Abe through the gates of death, leave the lies and the chains behind, and become free?"

I made a show of deep and serious thought. After a moment I took a deep breath and spoke quietly. "I guess I can understand where he is coming from. You grow sick of death, and of killing. It is a grotesquely banal thing. There is no glory or mystery to it. It is just ugly, and nauseating and unhappy." I nodded. "If he has found a way out, I'll follow him to the gate."

"Let me know when you are ready to make the payment. Then we can have sex and you can meet Abe."

She led me to the back door, opened it and let me out without saying goodbye. I stood in the sunshine a moment, looking up at the perfect blue sky, and told myself that if I ever wrote my memoirs, nobody would believe this one. Yet, looking at that sage green door, there it was, real. As real as the dismembered body I had seen at his villa.

I thrust my hands deep in my pockets and strolled slowly back to Guerrero Street, where I'd left my car. I had a bizarre sensation as I climbed behind the wheel, like there was somebody in my head, standing behind soundproof glass, screaming at me. It was like the feeling I'd had the day before, that there was something I had missed in Abe McGore's house. Only now that feeling was on steroids.

What had I missed?

There was the fact that they clearly didn't know yet that he was dead. What would they do when they found out? And would they connect my visit with his death? But I knew that wasn't it, and as I fired up the engine and pulled away there was another question in my mind: why hadn't the captain or the brigadier been in touch yet?

I cruised slowly back to the hotel, dropped off the car and made my way up to my room. There I called the brigadier.

"Harry, I'm glad you called."

"You could have called me."

"Yes, I was go—"

"In fact, the last I heard you and/or the colonel were going to call me last night."

"Indeed. I sent the colonel back to New York. Things have become somewhat more complicated than we at first thought."

"So our job hasn't been done for us?"

"I don't know. Things are not very clear at the moment, Harry. Can I ask you to stand by until we have finished a few more tests?" I drew breath to ask again but he cut me short. "Whatever you're going to ask me, Harry, the answer is going to be, I don't know."

"OK, listen, before you go, sir. I took a drive down to the United Church of Nergal this morning, on Guerrero Street."

"Oh, really?"

I told him what had happened and about the conversation I'd had with Anna Molyboha. He listened carefully till I had finished, then said, "Excellent. First rate. Do nothing. You understand? Go and visit a vineyard, have dinner, go to the beach. Kill time until I contact you. I'll be in touch this evening or tomorrow at the latest. Do not act on this. Understood?"

"Understood."

He hung up and I sat staring out at the midmorning sun through the window.

I WENT FOR A WALK, had some lunch, bought some books, went and stood looking out at the ocean, bought some clothes and returned to the hotel as the sun was losing its grip on the sky and slipping toward the horizon.

I went up to my room, showered and changed and ambled down to the dining room for an early dinner. It was as I was sipping my martini and looking at the menu that my cell rang. I didn't recognize the number.

"Yeah, Bauer."

"Mr. Harry Bauer?" It was a woman's voice. I thought of the brigadier, smiled to myself and said, "This is he."

"I have Mr. Salambek Bazurkaev on the line for you. Please hold."

I held and a mellow, agreeable voice with an accent that might have been Eastern European said, "Good evening. Allow me to introduce myself. My name is Salambek Bazurkaev—" He gave a small laugh. "I don't expect you to remember that. Most people call me Sam. I am Abe McGore's personal assistant."

"Good evening, it's good of you to call. I'll try to remember Salambek Bazurkaev, but if I draw a blank Sam—"

He cut me short and kept right on talking, with that agreeable smile in his voice. "Anna called me and told me about your very generous contribution and your interest in our church, and I just wanted to call and say thank you, and let you know that anything you want, and any doubts or questions you might have, please feel free to call me or Anna, any time." He injected a smile into his voice. "Anna is a fantastic administrator, and she is always ready to help. I myself will be in touch with Abe. Has he spoken to you yet?"

Suddenly my interest quickened, but I made it sound indifferent when I answered, "No, he hasn't, but I'd be fascinated to talk to him. He must be—"

"He is an amazing man. If he was a Hindu or a Buddhist they would say he was enlightened. He has certainly transcended ordinary human limitations. I will be talking to him soon and I know he will want to thank you personally. Have a great day."

"Yeah, you too. Thanks for calling."

I told the waiter to bring me a smoked salmon and avocado salad and a glass of cold Verdejo, followed by a sirloin steak medium rare and a half-bottle of whatever he recommended from the Napa Valley, as long as it was red and had plenty of vanilla from the oak. Then I sat and stared at my cell, wondering what the hell was going on.

FOUR

THE BRIGADIER TURNED UP THE NEXT MORNING AT seven AM. I had finished my exercise routine, was showered and dressed and waiting for my breakfast to arrive. It arrived with the brigadier, he gave the waiter ten bucks and wheeled the trolley in himself. He set it out on the balcony and poured two cups of coffee.

"Sit down, Harry. This is complicated."

I sat and helped myself to scrambled eggs, bacon and toast with plenty of butter. I offered him the serving fork and spoon but he shook his head.

"What's complicated?" I asked, cutting into the bacon. "Is the hand Abe McGore's?"

"The hand is Abe McGore's, yes. There is no doubt about that."

"So what's complicated?"

"What's complicated is that the head and the rest of the body are not."

I stared at him with the fork halfway to my mouth. I narrowed my eyes as I lowered the fork again, shaking my head. "That is insane..."

He took a deep breath and nodded. "These people, by which I

mean Eastern Europeans: Russians, Slavs, they have different standards and play by different rules. They..." He paused, looking into his coffee. "They really understand the meaning of all or nothing." He sipped and set down his cup. "We almost missed it. The ME happened to notice a slight discrepancy between one hand and another. He said they looked slightly wrong, and, in his words, for the sake of completeness he ran tests on both hands and found they belonged to different people. So he ran further tests on the body and on the head and found that everything, except the right hand, belonged to the same man. A man, incidentally, who is not in AFIS or CODIS, or any of the Five Eyes databases."

"But the facial recognition. You said it was a positive match."

"High probability, but on close examination we discovered the face had had extensive reconstructive surgery. It had also been badly damaged in the attack, as you saw for yourself. He—whoever he was—had been made to look like Abe McGore, but it wasn't him."

"Son of a bitch."

"Quite."

"So the job's not done."

"No. Very far from it."

"He's run. Why?"

"Best guess is that he somehow got wind that ODIN were looking for him."

"The Office of Demented Inbred Neophytes?" I said with unreasonable savagery.

"It can happen to the best. They are actually a very effective bunch. What is a little mind-boggling is what happened to his hand."

I nodded, trying to visualize it. "He's paranoid and he has a double. They were attacked. He got away but his double was killed. But then..."

I squinted at the brigadier and he supplied the final words.

"What happened to the double's right hand?"

I finished the scrambled eggs and wiped the plate with a slice of bread. But before eating it I grabbed my cup and leaned back in my chair.

"Why did I take his right hand?"

He frowned at me. "Clarify."

"If you were asked the question by the colonel, 'Why did Harry take the right hand?' what would you tell her?"

His frown deepened. "Well," he shrugged, "it was convenient. It was there, a manageable size, and had the double benefit of prints and DNA."

I nodded. "That is precisely—*exactly*—why I chose that hand. It was lying there, on the floor, at my feet, and I picked it up without thinking, for all those reasons."

"What are you saying, that it was a deliberate plant?"

"Nine investigators out of ten would have taken it as read that he was dead. One in ten would check the DNA and prints and leave it at that. One in a thousand would notice that the hands were slightly different and double-check. If it had been the cops instead of us, Abe McGore AKA Abbas Magomadov would now be officially dead. And that's the coldest trail there is."

He sighed. "As I said, They are very intense people, all or nothing. Who would have imagined..."

"He hacked his double to death, then had his own right hand cut off and planted there to fake his own death. He did something similar, but not so extreme, in Australia."

"Yes, you're right. I remember."

"His personal assistant called me last night. He said his name was..." I trailed off, trying to remember his name. "He said to call him Sam, but his name was Salambek, Salambek Bazurkaev."

"What did he want?"

"He wanted to welcome me to the church, thank me for my donation. He said Abe was going to call me. But then he told me *he'd* been trying to call Abe, but Abe wasn't answering his phone."

The brigadier pulled out his cell, stood and dialed a number.

Leaning with his backside against the balustrade he said, "Hi, It's Buddy. Listen, it's looking pretty much as if we are still in the game..." He listened for a moment, then said, "The hand was his but the rest wasn't. I'm having them send you the report as soon as it's complete. All the details will be in there. I'd like you to stay on this. I really don't want it getting into the hands of the Agency or the Bureau. Let's keep it in house.

"Now, meantime, I need to know all there is to know about Salambek Bazurkaev, he claims to be Abbas Magomadov's personal assistant. Will you try and find him? Perhaps send someone to chat with him. Let me know how you get on."

He hung up and studied me a moment.

"I'll get the techs on it right away. I'll bring you a laptop and give you an account number. You make a transfer of a hundred grand to their account. The numbers will show up for them, but they will be ghost numbers, there will be no transfer. We can do that. Get inside, Harry. Find out where Abbas is. Offer them more money, a second donation, if you think it will help. But find out what this church is about, and find Abbas. That man is dangerous. His focus on death and war is dangerous. At the very least it could end up being another Jonestown, at worst it could descend into terrorism."

"I hear you."

He stepped over to the sliding doors and paused there a moment, not looking at me, looking down at the floor.

"Couple of things before I go. There will be someone along this morning with the laptop, so best if you don't go out till that's been delivered. It will come to your room and the delivery agent will tell you it's a gift from Uncle Bud. You'll tell him that man doesn't know when to stop. Got it?"

"Got it."

"Go back to the church. You may find there are government agents there making inquiries about McGore. Be hostile to them and supportive of the church. Cultivate this Anna woman. See what you can get from her."

"OK."

"And, Harry, forgive me for saying so, but your relationship with Colonel Harris is becoming a nuisance. Sort it out, will you? Or one of you will have to go."

I gave a small nod. "We are going to meet in New York, when this job is finished."

"She should be involved in this job. I need her expertise. But I can't use her because you are the field operative. That means your personal relationship is interfering with our work. That's how lives are lost. It's not good enough."

"I understand."

"See to it, there's a good chap."

"Yes sir."

"Good man."

And with that he left.

I spent the next couple of hours reading a thriller about a world where it was always raining. After that I spent a while practicing combinations. Then at shortly before one there was a tap at the door. I opened it and a guy in a linen jacket and an agreeable face smiled at me.

"Mr. Bauer?"

"Yeah."

"I have a gift from Uncle Bud. Is this the right place?"

I nodded. "Yeah, that man doesn't know when to stop."

He handed me an attaché case and left. I carried it out to the table on the terrace and opened it. The computer was built into the case, and there was a very precise and detailed instruction manual. I spent the next half hour learning how to use it, and then called Anna. Her voice suggested there was more ice than control in her emotions.

"United Church of Nergal—"

"Anna, it's Harry."

"This is not good time—"

Apparently her grammar had shifted east too. "I want to make that donation. Can I come over?"

"There are men here."

"What are you talking about? What kind of men? What's going on, Anna?"

"Bad thing. I cannot talk."

"Are you at the church?"

"Yes, but don't—"

I hung up and went down with the attaché case to get my car, and twenty minutes later I was pulling up outside the sage green door on 23rd. There were two dark, nondescript SUVs parked outside and the door stood open. I grabbed the attaché case and went inside.

The small hallway was dark, and I could hear the roll and echo of voices inside the church. I followed the sound into the transept and saw that the office door was also open. I approached and stood leaning on the heavy, oak jamb. Inside, Anna was standing behind her desk, pale and drawn. She looked suddenly vulnerable. Somehow that made her more desirable than she had been the day before.

There were four men in suits. One of them was holding an open file, two of them had been rummaging in drawers and the fourth was sitting at the computer. Right then they had all stopped what they were doing to stare at me. I spoke quietly.

"What the hell is going on here?" To the guy who was standing holding the file I said, "Who are you?"

He arched an eyebrow. "I might ask you the same question."

"You might, and I might tell you to go to hell. See, I am a member of this church and I am entitled to be here without giving you a damned explanation. But from what I am seeing you are not members, so I am going to ask you one more time. Who the hell are you, and what the hell are you doing invading our members' privacy?"

He dropped the open file on the desk and pulled a leather wallet from his inside pocket. From it he took a plastic photocard and showed it to me.

"Jim Wallace, Office of the Director of Intelligence Networks.

We are attached to the Pentagon. These are officers Trent, Ruiz and Hoffman."

I examined the card, then looked at his face. "OK, that's who you are. Now I want to know, one, what the hell you are doing here, and two, what authority you have to be doing it? And let me just add, Officer Wallace, that if you have no authority to be here, either you leave, the cops kick you out on your asses, or I do."

His eyebrow strained to arch a little higher. "Ms Molyboha invited us in. There is no reason to get aggressive, sir."

I gave a humorless smile and narrowed my eyes. "Yeah, see? That is where we disagree. Ms Molyboha was raised in a regime where you don't tell government agents to go to hell. So when you boys showed up flashing your Pentagon badges she thought she had no choice but to let you in. And I am guessing you didn't do much to enlighten her as to the contrary. Am I wrong, Officer Wallace?"

"We are not required to do that."

"Right, well let *me* enlighten *you*. I was raised in the Bronx, and then spent eight years in special ops. So pick up your stuff and get the hell out of here. If you want some information on members, you get a damned warrant, you want information about the church you ask nicely. Get out."

They dropped the papers they were holding and moved toward the exit. I followed them. At the street door, as the other three filed out, Wallace paused and turned back.

"Do you know why we're here?"

"It was the first question I asked you."

"Are you a longstanding member?"

"No. I just joined. Is that relevant?"

"Maybe. You tell me your name, I'll tell you why we're here. I think you need to know."

"My name is Bauer. Harry Bauer."

He nodded. "Abe McGore was found murdered at his villa yesterday. It was a brutal murder. We are trying to locate his second in command, Salambek Bazurkaev, otherwise known as

Sam. He seems to have vanished. If you hear from him, give him my card and ask him to call. We need to eliminate him from our list of suspects."

He reached in his pocket and handed me his card. I took it and put it in my pocket.

"How come the San Francisco PD aren't handling this? Or the Feds?"

"That's a good question, Mr. Bauer. But I don't need to answer it." He pointed his finger at me like a gun. "You take care now. Those Chechens play rough."

I closed the door and went back to the office. She was sitting behind her desk, staring unseeing at its surface. I went and stood over her.

"Abbas is dead. Did you know about this?" Her eyes rose to meet mine, but she didn't say anything. I said, "When did you find out?"

Still she didn't say anything.

"Did you know yesterday, when I offered my donation?" Her eyes flicked to the attaché case on the floor by the desk. "Anna, *speak to me!*"

"No."

"No, you won't speak to me, or no—?"

"No, I didn't know!" She gestured toward the door, toward the lingering ghosts of the men who had left. "This, this is the first I have heard."

"Did you talk to Abe last night."

"He did not answer his phone."

"You spoke to Sam?"

"I call Salambek, I told him about your donation. He said he would call Abe. He could not find him either. So he call you."

"They said they can't find Salambeck either."

"I know."

I spread my hands and let them drop by my side. "I was so motivated. I thought I had found the way…" She was studying my face. She had no expression on her own. I went on. "I guess it's true. If you live by the sword, you die by the sword."

"That is gay bullshit," she said quietly.

"Yeah, well the facts seem to disagree with you." I paused, staring at her perfect, unfeeling face. "Anna, I am sorry, but you realize, with Abe dead and Salambek disappeared, I cannot make the donation. I was going to make a hundred grand now and another two fifty in a couple of months. But as things stand..."

She looked at the wall, biting her lip. I sighed, turned and picked up the attaché case.

As I stepped out through the door I thought I'd blown it, though I couldn't think of anything else I could have done. Yet, for some reason she hadn't taken the bait. But as I reached the transept, and paused to look down along the nave, where the huge candles were burning on the great silver candelabras, I heard her footfall behind me. I turned and saw her in the doorway, smiling a strange smile.

"Wait," she said. She came up beside me and took my hand. "Come, leave here the case."

I dropped it and she led me to the center of the floor, among the candles. Now she smiled, and I could see the flames dancing in her eyes. She reached up and kissed me, and whispered moist in my ear. *"Take off your clothes, and I will tell you some secrets..."*

FIVE

I LAY ON THE HARD STONE FLOOR, LOOKING INTO THE impenetrable shadows under the ceiling, listening to the echoes of her insane screams among the rafters, as she fell on the stone flags beside me. After a couple of minutes she got to her feet and started to pull on her jeans.

"Come," she said. "I must explain some things to you. Bring your case." And she walked away, half dressed, receding across the vast, cold, cavernous space.

I sat up, telling myself that had to go down in the archives as one of the most insane and least enjoyable encounters I had ever had. I pulled on my own jeans and followed her across the expanse of chilly stone.

In the office I put the attaché case on the desk and started pulling on my socks and boots.

"So what are these secrets you are going to tell me?"

She was sitting behind the desk buttoning her blouse. "First I need see your money."

I tucked in my shirt, spun the case, flipped the latches and turned it back to show her.

"You don't get to see a single cent. I'm not with the mob, I don't deal in dope. I haven't got that kind of cash. I was going to transfer a hundred grand to one of the offshore accounts you said you had, and another two fifty in a couple of months. But if Abe McGore is dead…" I shrugged, then held her eye. "What are these secrets, Anna?"

She stared at the computer in the case so long I was about to slam it shut and walk away. She must have caught my mood because she glanced at me with her eyes and said, "I can tell you something. But it must never leave this room. You can never tell nobody else. You agree?"

"Sure."

"And you will make transfer?"

"That depends on what you tell me, Anna. If you tell me Putin wears pink frilly panties, no deal."

She frowned real hard. "How can I know what panties Putin wears?" Clearly humor was not the big thing in Chechnya.

"It's a…" I sighed. "The money depends on what kind of secret you give me, Anna. That's the way it works."

"Abbas is not dead."

I aimed for something between stunned and incredulous. Apparently I pulled it off because she smiled. I pointed out at the door toward the street. "Four Pentagon officials just got through telling me they found his body yesterday."

"It is a long story, the story of Abbas's life, how he escapes death again and again. The man they found in his house was not Abbas. It is 'nother man. But Abbas must leave something of himself so that they believe it is him."

"Something of himself?"

"Yes. He leaves his blood, his DNK, no, DNA, he leave his right hand. These stupids find his hand and they believe it belongs to the body, destroyed body, and they conclusion that Abbas Magomadov is dead. But he is not dead. He will never die."

"Is he here, in the church? Can I see him?"

She pointed at the computer. "First one hundred thousand dollars. Then I talk to him. And if he want to meet you, I will come and have sex with you in your hotel."

I suppressed a confused frown and asked, "When?"

She leered. "You are in big hurry?"

I sighed again, then leaned across the desk and spoke savagely to her. "*I want to die, Anna! I am tired of suffering! I need this! Quit playing games!*"

"Tonight," she said, with the smile still playing on her lips. "Maybe I call you, maybe I come see you."

I sat at the desk, turned the computer to face me and rattled the information onto the screen. Then I crooked my finger at her. "Type in the account number."

She found it in a small, black book in the drawer of the desk, came round and typed it in while I looked away. When she was done I hit enter and after a moment said to her, "Check your account."

She went to the computer at the other desk and after a couple of minutes she turned and smiled at me.

"I think you have just become important member of church. If you are also a real man and a warrior, not a gay, then you have big future in church."

I didn't return the smile. I closed the attaché case and stood.

"What I want, Anna, is to meet this extraordinary man, to die and become liberated from my past, from the ghosts and the bonds that hold me down. Arrange that for me, and there will be a lot more, believe me."

I drove back to my hotel feeling slightly sick, not as though I would throw up, but like I wanted to purge myself of something unclean inside me. It was not a good feeling. I went to the hotel bar and ordered myself a Bushmills straight up and sat at the bar, eating peanuts and sipping the water of life. When I'd finished that one I ordered another and carried it and the peanuts to a table in the corner. I thought about calling the brigadier or the colonel to brief them on what had happened, but an irrational impulse, a feeling of anger and revulsion made me suddenly want to have nothing to do with them.

I looked at my phone and dropped it on the table, telling

myself I'd call one of them later, but feeling that I would not; that I might never call them again. I tried to rationalize the feeling, to make sense of it; but all I could think of was the colonel leaving without a word, the brigadier telling me, "Sort it out, will you?", and the dismembered body on the terrace, the man who had been hacked to pieces so that another man could live—and Anna looking over me, screaming. A voice in my head told me it was the inhumanity. The inhumanity of one human against another human.

But then I asked myself, what did we mean when we spoke about humanity? The fact of caring about other people? About their suffering? Was *that* what we meant by humanity? I scowled at my drink. Surely nothing could be less human than giving a damn about your neighbor. Surely the characteristic that defined the human race was the willingness to destroy other people in order to achieve our own purpose.

I saw my own, distorted reflection in my glass, looking back at me. And then, I thought, there was the exception to the rule: the stupid schmuck driven by some misguided sense of loyalty, who is willing to lay himself down and go through hell in order to serve somebody else's purpose, through loyalty.

But how rarely, how rarely was that loyalty reciprocated. How often it was repaid with cold indifference, and being sold down the river. I picked up my cell and stared at the screen, thinking about Dr. Claire Erickson in Pinedale, Wyoming. What about my loyalty to her? Was I really any better than the people I was so bitter against? Had I not sold her down the river for my own purpose?

I rubbed my face with my hands and told myself I was getting drunk. Then I told myself I didn't give a damn whether I was getting drunk or not. I was sick of...

Sick of what?

I didn't answer my own question. I drained my glass, stood and made my way up to my room.

I fell on the bed fully dressed and slept for a couple of hours or four. I awoke with a headache, realizing I hadn't had lunch. I pulled off my clothes and dropped them on the floor, and stood under the shower for fifteen minutes, turning the water from scalding to cold and back again. By the time I stepped out and started toweling myself dry, my head felt a little clearer.

I dressed and as I did so I told myself I had picked this job, and the brigadier had allowed me to become a rich man with his policy of spoils of war. He was not my father, or my nursemaid, he was my employer. And in any case, he was right, the stupid business with the colonel was interfering with her ability to work, and mine to move on.

I tucked in my shirt, rolled back the cuffs and called Claire in Pinedale.

"Wow, you called."

"Yeah. Are you mad at me?"

"No, just wondering. You talked a lot about moving here, the ranch, horses..." You could almost hear her shrug.

"It seemed like a pretty good idea at the time."

"Not anymore?"

"No, actually it seems like a better idea every day."

"Don't play games with me, Harry. I can forgive most things, but not that." I tried to answer, but I couldn't find the words. She went on, "You said you had to finish your work. You never told me what you do."

"I have never played with you, and I don't aim to start now. But I have probably been thoughtless, inconsiderate. I'd like to make up for that. Is it too late?"

"No, Harry. It's not too late."

"No howdy ma'am cowboys trying to move in?"

"There are plenty of cowboys in Wyoming, Harry. It *is* the Cowboy State. But I ain't steppin' out with none of them right now." There was laughter in her voice. I smiled.

"I guess I'd better stop dragging my heels then."

"Might be a good idea."

"I have a job I have to finish. Shouldn't be more than a few days. Then I have to go to New York for a..." I hesitated. "For a meeting. As soon as that meeting is finished, I'll climb in my Jeep and burn rubber for Pinedale."

"Are you serious?"

"Yeah, I'm serious, Claire."

There was another silence, but her voice was still carrying a smile when she said, "Well, I'm not going to start putting out welcome banners yet, because you *are* a little unpredictable, Harry Bauer. But I will say you've made my day."

"Yeah, you've made mine too." Then I added, "Claire?"

"Yeah?"

"I can't tell you exactly when, because I don't know exactly what I'm going to be doing over the next week. But I'll call you, in the next few days."

"That'll be nice."

"I'll see you soon."

I hung up and felt better about life.

The call came a couple of hours later. It was a guy with a pleasant voice. His English was good but he had a slight East-European accent. It wasn't Sam.

"Mr. Bauer?"

"Yeah, who's this?"

"My name is Bohdan Fedorko. You may call me Bob, if it is simpler. I am the chief administrator at the United Church of Nergal. Anna has asked me to call you."

"I thought she was going to call me herself."

"That was her original intention, Mr. Bauer, but circum-stances have changed a little. She has asked me to go and collect you at the hotel. She would like to meet you at the Retreat."

"The Retreat? What's that?"

"It is a country house that the church purchased partly as an investment, and partly as a retreat for members, where they can meditate and explore the teachings of Abe McGore, the Master."

"Will he be there?"

There was a protracted silence. Finally he said, "The Master is dead, Mr. Bauer. I thought you knew that."

"Yeah, my mistake. Anna will be there?"

"She will meet you there, yes. She asked me to tell you to prepare a suitcase for a few days. Will it suit you if I collect you in half an hour?"

"Sure."

I packed my leather bag, and while I was at it I strapped my Sig Sauer P226 under my arm, and my Fairbairn and Sykes to my ankle, inside my boot. Half an hour later I was down in the lobby, waiting for Bohdan Bob Fedorko.

He'd obviously been shown a picture of me because when he walked through the door he recognized me without having to go to the reception desk. I was sitting in a brown leather chair by a palm, and he walked right up, smiling. He was tall and strongly built, with very short blond hair and pale blue eyes. He had an easy smile and a courteous manner, but a closer look told you he'd break your neck without thinking twice if he had to.

"Mr. Bauer? I hope I didn't keep you waiting."

"You're right on time."

I followed him out to a dark SUV with tinted windows and he opened the sliding rear door for me. As soon as I was in he slammed it closed and a moment later he got behind the wheel and we pulled away from the hotel. As we moved in among the traffic, he spoke without looking over his shoulder.

"Please forgive the cloak and dagger, but a man like Abbas, who has had such an extraordinary past, attracts a lot of attention, and many enemies. For that reason it is best if as few people as possible see you are coming with me. So, the smoked windows..." He trailed off.

"Where are we going?"

"North, in the mountains above Point Reyes Station." He nodded like he was agreeing with a voice in his head. "Very beautiful up there. Very green."

"You're not Chechen."

He wasn't expecting it and glanced in the mirror for the first time.

"No."

"You're not Russian either."

"Why you are interested in my nationality? I am American." He spoke looking in his side mirrors, avoiding looking at me. The question had shaken him enough to affect his grammar.

I smiled. "I have a hundred thousand reasons to be curious. I am curious about the whole outfit. Everyone I've met so far has been Chechen, including the founder. Sam is Chechen, Anna is Chechen. But you..." I paused. "You were there at the computer when I first went to the church."

"Yes. I told you. I am the administrator."

"But you're not a Chechen."

"We have many members, over two thousand, and it is growing. Only a few of the oldest are Chechen. Others are from all over the world."

"Including Ukraine?"

It took him a moment to reply. "Some from Ukraine, not many."

"But that's where you're from, right?"

"Why you say that?"

"The accent. It's like Russian, only softer."

"Does it matter?"

He glanced in the mirror for the second time. I caught his eye and shook my head. "Not to me."

He smiled. "Me either."

I looked out of the tinted window at the Pacific Ocean sliding by as we crossed the Golden Gate. It didn't matter to me if he was Ukrainian or Chechen. But if anybody was likely to tear a Chechen war criminal into small pieces, it might just be a Ukrainian. It was the wrong war, I told myself. Abbas had fled Chechnya long before the Chechens helped Putin in Ukraine, but that didn't stop my imagination from creating various scenarios where this mild, pleasant Ukrainian took a battle axe to a man he thought was Abbas Magomadov.

And if he had, I told myself, I wasn't about to blow the whistle on him.

"Warriors," he said suddenly as we exited the bridge into the recreation area. He was watching me in the mirror again. "Warriors have no nation. We are a nation in ourselves."

I nodded a few times before smiling.

"That sounds great," I said, "but we both know it's bullshit."

He laughed out loud, and we didn't speak again until we reached the Retreat.

SIX

WHEN PEOPLE THINK OF CALIFORNIA, THEY TEND TO
think of Southern California's dry arid landscapes, palm trees and
white sandy beaches. But it is a long state, stretching from
Arizona in the south to Nevada in the north, and the north is
quite different to the south. It's green and fertile with an abun-
dance of trees, from oaks and sycamore to fir and of course pines.
There are green meadows swarming with yellow, violet and blue
flowers and, here in Marin County, where the Retreat was
located, there were lush green peaks and deep forests swarming up
their sides.

We stopped at a large, steel gate set in a twelve-foot wall. Bob
lowered his window, leaned out and waved at a camera sitting on
the column beside the gate. After a moment the gate began to roll
back and we rolled through.

The driveway wound first through woodland which obscured
the house from view, and then through a wide expanse of lawn,
dotted here and there with ponds and copses, which cast long
shadows in the late afternoon. Until we came at last to a Georgian
manor house with a large dome, colored copper by the sun, sitting
above the entrance. It was set among Italianate gardens and I
couldn't help feeling the brigadier would have approved.

Bob pulled up outside the broad steps that led to the door, and turned to look at me over his shoulder.

"I think she'll be waiting for you in back." I went to open the door but he stopped me with his voice. "Be ready to change your view on some things. She and Abe, they are pretty intense."

I paused with my hand on the door, then said, "Abe is dead, remember?"

"Sure."

I got out and climbed the steps as he drove away to where I figured the garage was. The door was open and I stepped through into a high, dark, echoing hall with a checkerboard floor. A flight of white, marble steps rose to a circular galleried landing beneath the dome, where shafts of light leaned in and illuminated well-fed women in various stages of angelic undress.

Sharp footsteps, half a second apart like the strokes of a ticking clock, approached out of the shadows, and a moment later I saw a man in a white jacket, with a white turban on his head. He was walking toward me across the black and white floor. He must have been six foot six, and had a long beard that reached down as far as his belly. He stopped six feet from me and regarded me with black eyes.

"You are Mr. Harry Bauer?"

"Yeah."

"You will please follow me."

I followed him past the foot of the marble staircase, down a long passage, through a ballroom and out onto a granite terrace which overlooked a sweeping lawn, a large pond and a copse of weeping willows.

In the middle of the lawn they had fixed up a black tatami. Sitting around it in the late-afternoon light were guys dressed in jeans, barefoot and bare-chested. At one end, on my right, was Anna. She was sitting on a chair watching two guys grappling with each other in the middle of the mat. They were still standing, but one guy had ducked down and had the other around the waist and was trying to take him down. They scrabbled for a moment, then fell in a heap. They groped and fumbled for a moment, then one of them tapped out. They stood, slapped each other on the back and joined the chorus.

I descended the steps and Anna watched me cross the lawn. As I approached she pointed at me.

"Take off your shoes and your shirt."

I was about to tell her to go to hell. But as I looked around at all the other guys, I figured that, if what I wanted was to get to Abbas Magomadov, that probably wouldn't be smart. So I pulled off my boots and stripped off my shirt. As I did so she said something in what might have been Chechen or Russian. A huge, bald guy who was sitting on her right got to his feet and leered at me. He had tattoos from his neck down to his belt, and all down his arms to his hands. Something told me he wasn't going to be my new best friend. Anna said:

"You will fight Bula. Only one rule in this fight. You must not kill him."

There was some scattered laughter. They made space for me to get through and I stepped onto the tatami. Bula walked like a man trying to find a way around his own muscles. His arms swung out from his body and his knees seemed to arc around his inner thighs. I smiled at him.

"At another time and in another place, Bula, we might have been friends."

I don't know if he understood me. I don't know if he understood anything. His neck swelled, he roared like a tyrannosaurus with an angry ferret up its ass and he charged at me. He wanted to take me down. He was five or six inches taller than me and weighed two hundred pounds more than I did. If he got me on the ground I didn't stand a chance.

The trouble with taking people down, though, is you have to drop your guard and get inside theirs before you can even start getting to work. So I didn't retreat. I slipped my left foot back and lunged at him like I was fencing, only instead of a foil to the heart, it was my right fist to his left eye.

That was about seven hundred pounds of combined weight, plus the thrust of his charge and my lunge, all concentrated onto my fist, with which I habitually break bricks, and his eye, which was soft and squidgy. I could have struck the tip of his jaw and ended the fight right there, but I knew they wanted a spectacle, an exhibition—and I figured they all needed a lesson.

Bula juddered to a halt and staggered. He didn't scream or cry out. He just put his hands to his eye and said, "Ah, ah..." I almost felt sorry for him.

With his hands to his eye his floating ribs, his solar plexus and his belly were wide open. I stepped in and drove a savage right hook into his floating ribs, a left hook to his liver and, as he doubled up, an upper cut to his face.

I backed up a couple of steps to see if he was finished. I figured his eye would be a problem, but he was an ox and he might just keep coming.

He stayed doubled over for a few seconds. I walked around him and looked at Anna. She held my eye, but as usual there was no expression. Bula stood erect with difficulty and turned to search for me. His left eye was badly swollen, red, and I could see a trickle of blood from the corner. His right eye said he was going to kill me, whatever the rules. He adopted a boxing position, left fist forward, and started to move in.

His reach was greater than mine. So I knew I had to avoid his jab. But with his left eye swollen up, all I had to do was keep moving slightly to my right of his fist, which was blind for him. As he tried to adjust I smashed a savage roundhouse with my instep into the side of his knee. He was tough. It didn't snap, but it hurt. So I did it again. And as my foot touched the ground I grabbed his arm above his elbow with my left hand and pounded his kidneys and his floating ribs with my right. He staggered a step forward and I delivered two front kicks to the back of his left knee. He stopped staggering and started hobbling.

I walked around to face him and looked him in his one good eye. I held up my left finger and he focused on it.

"Strength," I said, "is not everything," and I drove a right hook pile-driving through his jaw. His legs wobbled like dancing spaghetti and he dropped to the mat. Anna was staring at me. I stared back and said, "What did I do wrong?"

She didn't say anything so I looked around me. "What did I do wrong? That—" I pointed down at the heap of Bula on the ground. "That is not the warrior's way. So what did I do wrong?"

Nobody spoke. So I spoke more quietly. "I wasted time, and I put myself at risk several times so that I could offer you an exhibition. Fighting is not an exhibition. War is not an exhibition, unless you are a politician. For a warrior, it is a matter of life and death. My life, his death. And it needs to be finished as quickly as possible. You—"

While I was talking I had been looking at the assembled men. I chose the most dangerous looking one and pointed at him.

"Come here a minute."

He looked at Anna and she nodded. He stood and came to stand in front of me.

"I have right now five targets that will finish this fight in less than three seconds." I made a V with all four fingers and placed them at his eyes. "One—"

I made a vertical fist and placed it at the tip of his jaw. "Two—"

I rotated my hip and placed my left fist on his solar plexus, "three," shifted it and placed it vertical, in a left hook on his liver, "four," and finally I stepped back and placed my instep in his groin, "and five. Any one of these blows will finish a fight instantly." I turned to him and said, "Attack me."

He was a pro. He didn't get into guard and waste time shuffling around. His right foot went straight for my right knee. I blocked it with an oblique kick to his shin and as my foot touched the ground I jabbed into his eyes, retracted and smashed my fist into his jaw. As I pulled back I rotated my hip and drove a rear straight punch into his solar plexus, pulled back, twisted my left foot and drove the same fist in a hook into his liver. He staggered back and I smashed my instep into his balls. He fell with a thud on his back. The whole thing had taken less than three seconds.

I pointed to him on the ground. "That, is the warrior's way." I looked over at Anna. There was an expression on her face, but it was almost impossible to read what it was. Whatever it was, it was intense. I said, "Like I said, war is not an exhibition. Was there anything else you wanted?"

"Yes. Go inside. Akal will take you to your room. Shower—"

I was getting mad at being told what to do. I snapped, "I already showered."

Her chin lifted. "You will shower again. These are the steps you must take if you want to move to the next level."

"Fine. Akal takes me to my room. I shower. What then?"

"Meditate while you shower, Harry Bauer. These ablutions are so that you move to the next stage with a cleansed soul."

I nodded and glanced at the tatami, where Bula and the other guy were being revived. I wondered for a moment how this willowy girl who was teaching me how to get to the next level would have fared out there. I killed the sour thought, grabbed my shirt and my boots and made my way back toward the house.

Akal was waiting in the ballroom, watching me. It occurred to me that from where he was standing he would have seen the demonstration, and then seen me approach the house. For some reason that made me uneasy.

"Anna wants you to show me to my room," I told him.

"Please follow."

He turned and led me back to the hall and up the marble steps to the galleried landing. Below I could see the front door open and the dying light of the evening leaning in, making a sharp, luminous blade on the floor. A door opened out of sight, there was a voice far beneath us, a table or a chair was moved. All these echoes were gathered up and ricocheted, deformed and indistinct, into the dome above our heads.

We turned down a dogleg and followed the passage to the end.

Here Akal unlocked a large mahogany door and pushed it open. I stepped inside and he came in after me.

There was a huge, four-poster bed in carved oak. Double windows overlooked the lawn where straggling men were gathering up the tatami, while others sparred with flying kicks, or practiced katas. Anna and her chair had gone.

Akal opened a door onto an en suite bathroom, then turned and handed me the key to the bedroom.

"The ritual requires you to begin by meditating on the thousand natures of death. You seek to die like the snake, and shed your skin. So that after meditation the next step is to shower, and wash away your dead nature. Thus your new nature may become." He gestured to the bed where clothes had been laid out. "We will burn your old clothes. Your new clothes symbolize your new becoming."

I considered him a moment. My instinct told me he was a dangerous man. "Are you a warrior? You practice Gatka?"

He bowed slightly and looked at the floor. "I am merely a servant, sir. If there is anything you need, please ring on the bell and I will attend to you."

With that he bowed again and left the room. I put the key in the door and locked it, then examined the clothes on the bed. They were similar to the Shaolin Arhat robes, with a short jacket and loose pants secured at the ankle. The color was white.

I sat for a while on the bed, watching the sky grow dark outside. I wondered how long they expected me to meditate. I figured forty-five minutes would be about right, and then fell to wondering about the thousand natures of death. I could only think of one. There might be a million ways to approach death, but only one to die. You stopped living. Period.

That made me wonder what death actually was. I had seen it a thousand times or more, in many horrific ways. Sometimes it involved the partial or total destruction of a living being, but not always. Sometimes that living being retained its integrity, but something stopped, went away, became absent.

It struck me suddenly that it was an interesting thought, and that maybe after all there was something valuable in what Abbas Magomadov was doing. Perhaps he was right, and the only way for human beings to evolve and grow, was to die and re-become; a kind of reincarnation without actually physically dying.

I brought my mind back to the issue I was supposed to meditate on. The thousand natures of death. So perhaps one was destruction, the simple absence of life, and another was change and growth. I wondered if that was really what had happened to Abbas up in the mountains on the border with Georgia. Had he changed, evolved, shed his skin and become a different person?

Or was it all bullshit?

Either way, if destruction and change were two forms of death, that left nine hundred and ninety-eight more, and I was telling myself I did not have the patience or the inclination to go through nine hundred and ninety-eight natures of death.

But as I gazed out at the now dark parkland outside, I thought about Claire and Wyoming and the horse ranch, and I asked myself if after all I was so different to Abbas. Had I not devoted my life to killing? Where was "Thou shalt not kill" qualified as "Thou shalt not kill nice people, but it is OK to kill bad guys"? And had I not suddenly reached a time in my life where I had shed my own serpent skin and now wanted to raise horses, and perhaps children? Wasn't that a new life? And for there to be a new me didn't the old me—that daemon who only knew how to kill—didn't that need to die?

I sighed and went to shower, or ablute, or whatever the hell it was I was doing. And as I stood under the steaming water, far off, I heard the thud of a chopper approaching.

SEVEN

As I was toweling myself dry after the shower I heard the bedroom door open. I wrapped the towel around my waist and stepped out. There were three Japanese girls there in kimonos. They all bowed politely and one stepped up and removed the towel from my waist. After that they laid me on the bed, covered me in aromatic oils and gave me the best massage I have ever had in my life.

When they were done they dressed me in the clothes that had been left on the bed, bowed politely and left.

I was just writing a message to the brigadier which started, "Hello Mudda, Hello Fadda, here I am in Camp Granada," when there was a tap on the door. I sent the message, put the phone in my pocket and said, "Come!"

It was Akal. He bowed slightly and said, "The secretary asks that you join her downstairs in the drawing room, sir. With your permission I will arrange your bags."

"Sure, are we going somewhere, Akal?"

"The secretary has asked me to pack your bags, sir."

I left him to it and made my way downstairs feeling remarkably well, all things considered, and telling myself there must have been something in the oils. I found the drawing room without much difficulty, and inside it I found Anna sitting in a very large calico armchair beside a very large marble fireplace. She had what looked like a gin and tonic in her hand and pointed to a silver tray of decanters and bottles on the credenza.

"Have a drink. We have a few minutes."

I moved to the tray and poured myself a whiskey.

"How did the Japanese girls get in? I locked the door."

"They have pass keys to all the rooms. Did they not please you?"

"Very much. I just like people to knock."

"You were in the shower."

"How do you know?"

"I was watching you. You are in the church now, Harry. Different rules apply."

"Rules?" I sipped the whiskey. It was exceptional. I swallowed and said, "I don't like rules. It's why I was asked to leave the SAS."

I went and stood by the fire, looking down at her. She said, "I know. But give it time, Harry." She smiled, and I realized it was the first real expression I had seen on her face. "After your display this afternoon, you are not just a member, you are not a soldier, you are what Master Abbas calls a hero. Do you know what is a hero?"

"Yeah, it's a myth."

She laughed. It shocked me. It was a warm, human sound emitting from an iceberg. "A myth? And tell me, my hero, do you know what is a myth? You have the blindness of the decimal era, the post-Roman blinkers who believe only in three dimensions. The Master will open your eyes, but I will tell you this, a hero is a child of the gods. The heroes are the children of the Elohim and they carry the blood of the gods in their veins. A hero has the divine fire in his blood, and he may become a god."

I sipped the whiskey and held her eye while I rolled the nectar around my mouth. After I had swallowed and smacked my lips I asked her, "You believe that? Because I have to tell you, to me it sounds like bullshit. There are no gods, Anna, and there are no heroes. There are bad people and there are less bad people, we are all driven by either the desire for what we haven't got, or the desire to get away from what we have got—most often it's both. So we are all basically selfish. Only sometimes what we want benefits others, sometimes more and other times less."

"Life has been cruel to you."

I nodded. "And I have been pretty cruel to life, too."

"Everyone who comes to the Church of Nergal comes from that place, driven by a desire to die, and be reborn. Now tell me something, Hero, if you can achieve your dream of rebirth, who would you want to be? What would be your nature?"

I actually thought about it. This whole subject of death and rebirth was getting to me. I frowned and spoke half to myself. "I would want to be compassionate..." I thought of the head on the table in Abbas's house, grinning savagely at the sinking moon: humanity and inhumanity. "I would want to be more humane, capable of real empathy."

"So, you believe these qualities exist, but you do not believe yourself capable of them." I didn't answer. I just frowned at her. She went on, "So you, now, as you live, are characterized by a belief in yourself as somebody limited and ineffectual. That image of yourself must die. You must be reborn, believing in your capacity for empathy and compassion. You must believe in yourself as a hero, with the capacity to be a god."

I wanted to tell her she was out of her mind. Instead I said, "Have you done that?"

"I am not a hero."

"What about Abbas?"

"He has transcended. He is a god."

Before I could laugh there was a knock at the door. It opened and Akal stepped in. "The plane is ready, Lady Secretary."

She stood. "Give me your cell."

I shook my head. "No."

"Where we are going, you cannot take your cell. You must leave it here." She held out her hand. "Otherwise you cannot go."

I knew I had no choice. I also knew my cell was virtually impossible to break into. So I handed it over. She gave it to Akal and said, "Let's go."

I followed her out into the night. Through the open front door the porch lights reflected dimly off a Range Rover. Bhodan Bob Fedorko, who had collected me from the hotel, was holding the rear door of the car open. Anna climbed in and I went round and got in the other side. As I settled next to her I asked, "Akal said the plane was ready. What plane?"

"Always questions."

"Yeah, always questions. What plane?"

Her eyes flicked over my face. There was almost a smile at the corner of her mouth. "If we are going to fly, we need a plane."

"Unless we are gods."

"Some gods need planes. It depends what kind of a god you are."

Bob climbed behind the wheel. The door closed with a muted thud and we took off.

We didn't follow the drive. We went round back of the house and followed a track across the sweeping lawns. We passed a large copse and descended a hill into deep darkness, where only the amber wash of the headlamps was visible, moving ahead of us, picking out the occasional skeleton of a tree, or the clutching fingers of branches. But after a while the distant glimmer of a handful of lights showed in the night air. And as we drew closer I saw there was a floodlit area where the graceful shape of a Gulfstream stood on a strip of tarmac.

I looked at her. Her eyes were on the plane. Her expression was, as always, hard to read, though the excitement was unmistakable.

"Where are we going?"

She glanced at me and frowned, like I'd interrupted her while she was counting.

"We are going to meet Abbas. You know that. Why ask?"

I leaned toward her as the vehicle came to a halt. "I didn't ask you, what are we going to do? I asked you where. Where are we going, Anna?"

"Are you scared?"

I shook my head. "No."

"Then enjoy the ride, and stop asking useless questions."

Bob pulled the door open for her and she climbed out. I climbed out my side and followed her across the tarmac toward the plane.

Inside, it was as luxurious as you would expect, all toffee-colored leather and highly polished wood. She sat at a table and pointed at the seat opposite. I sat, the door closed and moments later the engines rose from a high-pitched whine to a scream. Then we began to move, hurtling through the darkness until suddenly we were weightless, and the dark world fell away beneath us. Small lights appeared momentarily through the portholes, then drifted out of sight.

I said, "We're headed south."

She nodded once.

"Panama?" I tried to read her face. There wasn't much written there, but what there was said no. "Not Panama, then Mexico."

The corner of her mouth twitched. So we were going to Mexico to meet Abbas Magomadov, author of three massacres. It wasn't especially surprising, but it made me wonder who was luring whom into a deathtrap.

Once we were airborne and we'd leveled off, they brought us drinks and a meal. We ate in silence and when she was finished Anna closed her eyes, signaling the end of any conversation that might have arisen.

After an hour and a half we began to descend. Looking out the window I could see the Pacific, bright with moonlight, and in the distance a dark stretch of land. So we were over Baja. Thousands of miles of empty desert, far enough from Sinaloa for there to be no crime and minimal law enforcement, remote enough to be virtually invisible, and yet close enough to California for easy, convenient access.

Pretty soon the dark desert was skimming past beneath us. Anna opened her eyes and looked out the window, and next thing we had hit the tarmac, the tires squealed and the turbines screamed. We slowed, then taxied to a halt. Anna smiled at me. "Welcome to Eden," she said, and there might have been menace in her eyes.

The stewardess opened the door and lowered the steps. Anna exited and climbed down. I stopped at the top and looked around. I could smell the salt on the air, and the breeze carried the sigh of surf. The runway was floodlit. Ahead of me was a rough structure that, by its shape, and the radar on the roof, obviously served as a tower. Lights glimmered inside, and parked outside it were two Land Rovers. One of them had its headlamps on and Anna crossed toward it while a couple of guys started unloading the luggage from the belly of the plane.

I trotted down the steps, and glancing over my shoulder I caught sight of the ocean about a mile away, glowing under the setting moon. I heard a car door slam and made my way to where the Land Rover was waiting with Anna in the back.

As I climbed in and sat next to her I said, "Baja."

She nodded.

"The church has a house here?"

"No. We have a town here. It is called *Nuevo Edén*."

"New Eden."

"This is Nergal Airport." The truck started to move away from the sea, along a track into the desert. "We will now go to the town."

"You built the town yourselves?"

"Yes."

"This has been tried before, you know? At least twice. Bhagwan Rajneesh tried it in Oregon, and Jim Jones in Guyana. Neither of those experiments worked out real well."

She watched me a while without speaking as we moved through the desert. Up ahead I saw a scattering of lights come into view. I jerked my head toward them.

"Is that downtown Nergal?"

"Is that supposed to be a joke, Harry?"

I sighed. "All of this is a joke, Anna. The airport, the town, the heroes, the gods—"

"You use your sarcasm as a defense. You say it has been tried before, twice. And you give me the example of a depraved Indian guru and a Christian psychopath. Do you know how many cities and major towns there are in the world, Harry?"

"'Course I do. I just don't remember right now."

"There are over four million. And each one of them—*each one of them*—started like this. Athens, Cairo, New York, London, San Francisco..."

"You going to name all four million of them?"

"They *all* started as small settlements guided by a strong leader."

"Yeah, but the ones that prospered were located with an eye to food and water, trade and defense, not hiding from authority in order to do weird rituals involving life, death and sex."

She frowned. "What am I hearing? Are you turning chicken? Why all this negative shit now?"

"A lot of people, more than you would imagine, have died needlessly because they chose to pretend things were OK when they weren't. I came to you in San Francisco, looking for a philosophy and a practice to help me recreate myself. Now you're talking to me about heroes becoming gods, bringing me to New Eden, hidden in the desert on the doorstep of Sinaloa country... All I'm telling you, Anna, is this had better be good. So far it stinks of crazy."

Her eyes flicked over me, up and down. "Sometimes you full of shit, Mr. Hero."

We pulled into what was more a settlement than a village. There were no roads as such. It was just the beaten earth between wooden, A-frame houses with gabled roofs, chimneys and small backyards, each with its own picket fence. The houses were centered around a large square in the center of which a lawn was struggling to grow. The whole place was still and silent, and the only light came from the windows of the houses and our headlamps.

We turned into one of the roads, climbed a slight hill and came to a large, two-story building surrounded by a palisade. We entered through a gate that stood open, and we pulled up outside the door. The gate swung closed behind us.

I climbed out and stood a moment looking at the house. Seven broad wooden stairs ascended to a deep porch with a solid balustrade. At the center there was a heavy, wooden door and at either side light filtered out through windows that were partially covered by drapes.

Anna brushed past me and climbed the stairs. The door opened before she reached it and an attractive young woman in a French maid's uniform bowed and stepped back to let her in. I smiled to myself and followed her up and into the house.

There was a small area that acted as a kind of open-plan entrance, and beyond it was a space that was reminiscent of a Viking hall. It had wood-paneled walls, a great fireplace on the far wall, a huge, heavy oak table in the center with twelve chairs set around it and, on the walls, animal skins and heads. Beside the fire, and looking oddly incongruous, were several armchairs and sofas. I half expected to see a Viking in bearskins sipping a martini.

The French maid left and tottered up the stairs to the upper floor, and Anna crossed the room to the fire, where she stood with her back to the flames, removing her coat. I went and sat on the arm of one of the chairs, watching her.

"What now?"

"Now we wait," she said.

"For what? And for how long?"

"For the Master. And as long as it takes."

I looked around and spotted a tray of drinks. I went and fixed myself a whiskey. "I'm not that good at waiting." I turned and saw she was looking at me. "I figure I'll have a nightcap and then I'll ask that cute maid to show me to my room."

"I am not sure," she said after a moment.

"What about?"

"Whether you were an inspiration, or the worst mistake I have ever made."

I smiled and sipped my whiskey. "Well, if I am the worst mistake you ever made, it's too late now. So there's no point worrying about it."

He didn't come down that night. His French maid came and told us the Master would see us in the morning. After that Anna went up and I sat and finished my whiskey.

EIGHT

I WAS AWOKEN BY A LOUD HAMMERING ON THE DOOR. I looked at my watch on the bedside table. It was five AM. I swung out of bed and went and opened the door. The light in the corridor was on and there was a guy in soldier's uniform a couple of doors down banging on Anna's door. I didn't speak so much as growl.

"What the hell do you want?"

"You dress now! We have meeting at Temple of Nergal! Dress now!" I didn't move because I was wondering whether to tear his head off and spit down his throat or shove his Heckler and Koch 416 up his ass and pull the trigger. He must have sensed my thoughts because he started striding toward me with an ugly face, bellowing at me, "Go! You go! Dress now!"

I had kind of settled on the Heckler and Koch alternative when Anna's door opened. He stopped just out of reach and turned to look back at her. She glanced at me, then spoke to him quietly in what sounded like Russian. He listened, then turned to face me and said, "Put on clothes. Master is talking in the temple in half hour."

I said, "What's your name, soldier?"

"Sergeant Igor Polachova, of the Palace Guard."

I nodded. "Good. Screw you, Igor."

Anna spoke quickly to Igor as she hurried toward me. She pushed me back into my room and Sergeant Polachova toward the stairs. She closed the door and pushed me again toward my bed.

"You are stupid!" she said, like she meant it. "Why you do these stupid things? Get dressed!" She opened my wardrobe and started throwing Chinese clothes at me. "Get dressed now, quickly. I will come for you in fifteen minutes, stupid!"

I put on the stupid Chinese uniform and went downstairs to the big room. The fire had burned down but the embers were still giving off a warm glow. A couple of lamps had been switched on, but the room was gloomy and sleepy.

A tray of coffee had been set on the big table and I helped myself. Five minutes later Anna came down on angry little feet and glared at me.

"Why did you not wait for me?"

"I have too many damned people telling me what to do right now. Have some coffee and relax."

"You have no discipline!"

"That's right."

She poured coffee and sipped it, flicking her eyes at me like it worried her that I had no discipline. I ignored her and went and stood on the porch. The sky wasn't even thinking about dawn yet, but there was a glow rising from the village, and small groups of people were walking through the dark streets, making their way to the main square.

Anna came and stood next to me. I reflected for a moment that it is always the most hostile people who end up being the most clingy. I spoke half to myself:

"If I were a god, I'd have people come and listen to me at ten AM, after I'd had breakfast."

"That is why you are not a god."

I looked down at her and smiled. "How do you know I am not a god?" She looked genuinely surprised and opened her mouth to answer, but I cut her short. "Have you got the criteria to make that assessment? How do you know..." I leaned down toward her and spoke in a stage whisper, "How do you know that I am not the real Abe McGore? How do you know I am not Nergal?" I chuckled and looked back at the straggling crowds. "You, Anna, don't know shit."

Eventually, as the last of the stragglers reached the square below, I finally agreed to follow Anna to the temple. I wanted to be the last to arrive. I couldn't have told you why, maybe it was just bloody-mindedness. But I had a feeling that if I was going to get close enough to Abbas to take him out, I was going to have to be enough of a pain in the ass to get into his inner circle.

His talk was going to confirm that theory for me.

The temple was a very large, open structure on the edge of the village, just beyond the main square. At a rough guess I figured it had to be five or six thousand square feet. It had a broad, low pyramid roof supported on wooden poles. The sides were open, but had tarps that could be dropped in case of cold, wind or rain. Right now they were open onto the blackness of the desert.

The wooden floor was strewn with rugs and cushions, and at the far end there was a dais, a kind of wooden box with a couple of steps up, and on top there was a large, wooden throne, made comfortable with cushions and rugs.

There must have been a thousand people there when we stepped inside. They were all sitting on the floor looking up at the dais and the empty chair. A few people glanced at us as we entered, and there was mild reproof in their eyes. We found a place and sat cross-legged, on a mat.

Five minutes later Abbas arrived. He was escorted by nine men in battle fatigues, all carrying HK416s. They surrounded the dais, three at the back and three either side, and he ascended the steps to the throne, where he sat and looked out at his faithful. There was absolute silence. In my gut I felt a hot surge of anger and frustration, which I fought to suppress. After a moment he held up both hands, palm out, and I saw that his left hand was prosthetic. He started to speak.

"Blessings to you, warriors. If rising at five in the morning is the greatest challenge you face this year, then you will be lucky warriors indeed."

There was some scattered laughter, but he didn't smile.

He let his left hand fall into his lap and turned his right hand back and forth a couple of times.

"I come to you this morning, before the rising of the sun, to talk to you about violence. We who are warriors deal in violence. It is our stock in trade. We create violence, we store violence, we sell it as a product and as a service, and we use it to achieve what we want in life."

He paused, looking around the room. His face was impassive. His eyes were expressionless. You couldn't help getting a feeling of deep peace from him, which was kind of unreal considering the things he was saying.

"But," he went on, shaking his head slightly, "What is violence? Can anybody tell me what is violence? I am sure there is not a man or women present here this morning who cannot show me what is violence, but how many understand it and can explain it?"

He didn't wait for an answer. He went right on.

"If I strike you with my hand or my foot, with a stick, a sword or an axe, if I shoot you with a gun or drop a bomb on your house or your city, where is the violence? The violence is not in me." He paused, looking around. "Sophistry? Philosophical bullshit? No." He'd had his right hand raised all the while. Now he laid it in his lap. "If the violence were in me, then I would be cowering, screaming, crying on the floor, begging for pity. But I ask you to think, *where* is the heart pounding? *Where* is the adrenaline burning? *Where* is rational thought lost? Where is fear causing incontinence, pissing and diarrhea? For, wherever these things are, that is where the violence is. Violence—and if you will be a warrior then you must assimilate this truth deep into your being—violence is in the victim. Violence is *how a person reacts to a word or an action*. Understand this, and you understand everything."

He took his time gazing at his faithful, engaging people's eyes, then moving on. Finally he drew breath and sighed softly.

"Violence is rooted in fear. Fear is the most powerful emotion that a human being can feel. Fear will make a mother sacrifice her baby, a man sacrifice his wife. Nothing is stronger in the human heart than pure, incontinent terror. Dignity, honor, love, all dissolve into tears, piss and diarrhea in the face of true terror.

"So violence, my warriors, is the act of generating fear in the mind and body of another person. You can do this by beating them or injuring them, or you can do it by threatening them with mutilation or death. There are many ways of striking fear into a person. Sometimes—" And now he smiled. It was a smile that was deep and cruel, and as dangerous as thin ice. "Sometimes simply being present is enough to cause real fear.

"Of course violence is not only fear. It is also physical and emotional pain. If I cause physical or emotional pain in a person, that person is living violence. And if you think about this for just a moment, then you understand that he who owns violence, he who can inflict real fear and pain, has real power. And the more fear and pain he is known to inflict, the more power he has."

His smile broadened. "Why," he said, gesturing to himself with his left hand, "Why am I sitting on this throne, teaching you? Because, my warriors, I am the man who can inflict the most pain and fear in this town. I *own* the violence in this town. And if Sinaloa are not kneeling at my feet this morning, it is only because they do not yet know who I am."

He gazed out at the darkness across the heads of his faithful and licked his lips, like he was savoring and digesting his own thoughts.

"Violence," he said at last, "the ability to inflict violence, is the single most valuable commodity on this planet. Nothing is more valuable. Oil, gold, heroin, sex, nothing comes close to the value —the intrinsic value—of the ability to inflict violence. This is why Moses tells his faithful 'Thou shall not kill,' and God tells his faithful, 'Vengeance is *mine*' not yours, *mine! You* must not kill, *I* will kill, or I will authorize you to kill, but if you kill, you will kill in *my name!* And *you* shall not seek vengeance or retribution. Vengeance is *mine.* I can authorize you to seek revenge, but only in *my* name!' And every crown, every pope, every president and emperor in history has played the same game. You," he stretched out his hand to point to his followers, "You may have the land and the crops to keep you busy, you can have the shops and the industry and the taverns and the whole, fucking circus—you can have it all! But the *violence! The violence is mine alone to dispense! And let him who tries to steal it from me beware, for my vengeance will be terrible!"*

He pointed down into the crowd at his feet. "But, how do we become masters of violence? It is not enough to be a skilled fighter. Something more is necessary. If I say to Bill, you, you, Bill: Bill, stand up and kick Charlie to death..."

He paused. There was a terrible silence. Slowly, jerkily, a young blond fellow got to his feet, staring from Abbas to the man sitting next to him and back again. Abbas showed him the palm of his hand. "Wait. Pause. Observe, all of you, how I have wielded violence here. You are all affected. Your hearts have accelerated, your adrenaline is flowing, you are scared and excited in equal measure. But how do you think I feel?" He didn't wait for an answer. It was a rhetorical question. "And if I now say to Bill, go ahead, kick Charlie to death. Kick him, stamp on him, stamp on his head, on his ribs... Of course Charlie will experience terrible violent feelings of fear and stress and anxiety. But if we look at Bill, we will see the same emotions in him. They are *both* victims of violence." He paused a moment, then, "Sit down, Bill. Nobody will die this morning, during this talk.

"The man who acquires the power to inflict violence, is the man who can rise above his own emotions, observe them from a place of detachment, and still the storms in his mind and in his organs. The man who can unleash screaming terror in another, while retaining absolute equanimity in his own emotional world, a steady pulse, a normal flow of adrenaline and a calm, clear mind.

This is the man who knows himself, who is slave to nobody, who knows the true meaning of, 'I am.'"

He paused again and looked around at the staring, transfixed faces. "Some of you may, in the secret places in your hearts, feel that what I say is barbaric or cruel. I shall not answer that except to ask you, truly, is there anything in what I have said that is not true? When you step outside the fantasies and constructs of human society, and you look at the real universe that nature has created, is there anything in what I have said that is not true?" He sat back. "Go now, have your breakfasts, your coffee and your bacon and your eggs, and at half past eleven we will gather at the sports field. Today, my warriors, you will meet death. Be at peace."

They all started to rise. I got to my feet and saw that he was staring straight at me. He pointed and crooked a finger, indicating I should go to him. As the crowd started to thin I pushed my way through them and made my way to the dais. I didn't wait to be invited up. I climbed the steps and stood in front of him. His eyes were like lasers fitted with microscopes.

"Who are you?"

"My name is Harry Bauer."

"I did not ask you your name. I know your name. I am asking who you are."

I gave him the kind of answer he deserved. I said, "There is no answer to that question, Abbas, unless I tell you, I am I."

"You call me Abbas?"

"Isn't that who you are?"

He gave his head a small shake. "I am the Master. What do you want from my church?"

"Peace."

"You come to a church that venerates a god of war, in search of peace?"

I sighed. "Come on, Abbas, quit playing games. I'm not one of your fresh-faced schoolboys or your damaged recruits from Chechnya or Russia. I was eight years in the SAS. I know what violence is and I know what death is. And we both know that there comes a time in your life when you need to make sense of it. From what I hear you've been there, and you've done it. I'm not going to fall on my knees and call you a god. I don't believe in gods. But I do believe you have had some kind of..." I searched for the word, surprised to discover that I actually meant what I was saying. Momentarily wrong-footed by my own mind, I fumbled and blurted out, "...a shift in consciousness or..."

He smiled, "Enlightenment?"

"They talk about that in Buddhism. I don't know what that is. But whatever it is I am prepared to pay, if that's what it takes. I've already paid you a hundred grand."

"And you are prepared to pay another two hundred and fifty thousand dollars." His face suddenly broke into a laugh. "But if I give you the secret now, maybe you won't pay the rest of the money!"

"If you are enlightened, you know that's not true. When I give my word, I follow through."

He became serious. "I believe you do." He looked away, toward the horizon where the sky was turning a dark blue-gray. "This is not a thing that you can pass from one person to another, Harry. This is..." He trailed off, then smiled and pointed at me. "Did you ever, when you were a kid, have a friend who saw an image somewhere—maybe a face in some peeling paint or plaster, a cat in the soot in a fireplace, a rabbit in the clouds—and they tried to make you see it, but it was no good? You just could not see what they saw. And then somebody said, 'Oh, the eye is here,' or 'it's tail is up there,' and that one clue was enough and suddenly the whole picture became clear? You have had that experience."

"Sure."

"This is the same. Something snaps, something clicks, and suddenly you see clearly what you have been looking at all your life."

"What?" I shook my head, not in the negative but in the frustration of not understanding. "What did you see?"

"The great joke," he said, and laughed again. "The huge, terrible, *absurd* cosmic joke. I can tell you, there is no right, there is no wrong, there is no death, there is no pain...," he shrugged, "but it will mean nothing to you, unless you see the cat's eye."

He stood and stepped down from the throne to stand right in front of me. "Skirnir, on an errand for one of the gods, when warned about a dangerous giant, replies, 'Fearlessness is better than a faint heart for any man who sticks his nose out of doors. The length of my life and the day of my death, were fated long ago.' We have no free will in the three-dimensional universe, Harry. We only have free will in the two-dimensional universe."

He chuckled and descended the steps of the dais. There he stopped and looked up at me, and I had the strange, sickening sensation that he knew exactly who I was.

"Did you ever hear about the man who was trapped in a vast mansion with infinite rooms, and he was running from one room to another desperately searching for himself?"

I nodded. "Yeah, I heard that one."

"That is the eye of the cat, Harry. I will see you later at the games."

He left with his nine guards and I watched him walk along the dusty track toward the big house. I noticed Anna, standing by one of the posts, watching me.

The eye of the cat, that gave everything meaning. I sighed and crossed the huge floor to where she was waiting.

NINE

I RETURNED TO MY ROOM, SHOWERED AND DRESSED, and returned downstairs to have breakfast. It had been set out on the long, heavy wooden table. The sideboard was laden with bacon, mushrooms, deviled kidneys, eggs—fried and scrambled—toast, croissants, butter and three types of jelly.

I had a feeling I was probably going to need to be light on my feet in a couple of hours, so I had some black coffee, a couple of rashers and a couple of eggs. While I was helping myself Anna came down. She stood in the doorway staring at me for a moment, till I looked up at her and said, "If you're trying to take my appetite away you're wasting your time."

"I don't care about your appetite."

"Sergeant Bradley, in the Regiment, we called him Kiwi because he was from New Zealand. He had this theory that you could draw a line from the Netherlands south to Italy, and everyone east of that line was autistic. His reasoning went something like: "They're all so fuckin' *literal! All of 'em!* You say, 'Go screw yourself,' they say, 'I sink zis vill hurt.' I told a guy, 'Get off my fuckin' back, Boris!' He says, 'I am sittink on my chair, ent my name is Peter. Everysink you get wrong!' They take everything *literal!*"

I looked at her beautiful, sulking face, sighed and sat down to eat.

"Why he spoke to you privately?"

I sipped my coffee, watching her over the rim, and told myself, *Be literal.*

"It was private."

"I am secretary."

"You're in love with him."

"That is ridiculous."

"No, it's stupid. Loving a man like Abbas can end in only one of two ways."

"What ways?"

"Tears or death."

"Three ways," she said quietly. "It can end in both."

I forked bacon and eggs into my mouth and spoke with my mouth full. "There are other options, you know."

"No."

"You could stop being stupid, leave this church and make a happy, normal life."

"*That* is stupid. My future is with the Master."

"Your choice, sister."

"I am not your sister."

I rolled my eyes and thought of Bradley.

At eleven twenty we made our way to an area of sand that had been cordoned off at the side of the temple. It was already packed with people. There must have been a thousand of them at least. Maybe a hundred of them were sitting around a large tatami that had been pegged down and cordoned off with ropes. They sat cross-legged, barefoot and bare-chested.

What looked like a large Persian rug had been laid at one end and a wooden throne had been set on the rug. Four chairs had been placed, two at either side of the throne. Anna led me to one of them and she sat beside me. Shortly afterwards Bohdan Bob Fedorko arrived, he greeted us and sat on one of the chairs at the far side of the throne.

"Whose the fourth one for?" I asked Anna.

"Salambek Bazurkaev, Sam, but he is not here."

"Where is he?"

"I don't know."

"Nobody knows."

She turned her head and stared me in the face for a moment. Finally she said, "Somebody knows."

"Do you know?"

"I just told you I—"

"Maybe you're lying."

"I don't know where he is. You ask too many questions. You are not respectful." Her voice was a harsh whisper. I smiled and held her eye. "People who kill as their profession, Anna, are by definition not respectful. And if they want to stay alive, they ask too many questions. Now you," I tapped her chest with my finger, "you are too respectful, and you don't ask enough questions. One of these days, I might have to save your life."

"Stupid," she said, not for the first time. But it lacked conviction.

Shortly after that Abbas arrived. He was wearing a long, white robe. His fine, sandy hair was loose around his shoulders and, with his beard, he looked like some kind of wannabe Jesus Christ. I wondered if it was intentional or unconscious. Everybody stood and saluted by slamming their right fist to their heart. He echoed the gesture more gently and sat. Everybody else sat too.

"Today," he spoke loudly and his voice echoed across the field. "Today we start a new chapter, and we rise to a new level. Today, in the words of the great Li Jun Fan, we begin honestly to express ourselves. We have dropped our chains and our shackles and today we are free. Is there anybody here who does not believe we are free?"

Total silence greeted his answer. He smiled.

"Jack," he said, "Jack Lee, stand. Enter the ring."

A guy halfway down on my left stood. He looked Korean, and his name suggested he was. He had the loose, dynamic stance that signals a seasoned Tae Kwon Do practitioner. He climbed through the ropes into the tatami and bowed to Abbas.

"Wolfgang, stand. Enter the ring."

A guy roughly opposite Lee stood. He was everything you would expect a German to be: six-three or four, built like a brick shithouse, with very short blond hair and pale blue eyes. He gave a small bow to Abbas, climbed through the ropes and settled to staring at Lee.

Abbas spoke again, but his voice had changed. There was a deadness to it.

"Today we celebrate our freedom by doing whatever the hell we like. Today we shall select the best of the best as the head of our personal guard. My two best, most beloved warriors will fight. The man who wins becomes my right-hand man, my most trusted lieutenant." There was a long pause. Then he added, "The other goes, without shame, to Valhalla."

The air seemed to turn icy. I examined Wolfgang's face, then Lee's. They had gone rigid. Finally Wolfgang turned to stare at Abbas, seeking confirmation. Abbas nodded once.

"Now we are free, Wolfgang. Now we do what always we have dreamed of. Now we play with death, and we lose our fear. You will fight to the death. The prize goes to the survivor, Valhalla for the loser, if he fights with courage." He gestured at them with both hands. "Begin."

There was no preamble. A gong sounded and Wolfgang moved fast to the center of the ring. Abbas spoke to me with his eyes on the two fighters.

"Who is your money on, Harry?"

Lee had shifted his right foot forward. He'd gone into a slight crouch and moved sideways. He had his right fist forward, aimed at Wolfgang's chin. His left hand was poised, loose under his own; and he circled Wolfgang to the right. I knew his style. He might have trained in Tae Kwon Do from the age of four, but he used the same style I used: no style. I said:

"A thousand bucks says Lee kills the German."

Abbas smiled. It was a complacent smile.

Wolfgang knew Lee would seek out the angles. He didn't have Wolfgang's reach, so he had to dodge from side to side and try to get inside his guard. In any direct attack Wolfgang would always come off best and he knew his own advantage was in straight, long-range blows. So he cut off Lee's circling by cutting across his path, and steadily backed him into a corner where he couldn't seek out the angles.

Then he closed in.

Lee had nowhere to retreat to and his head was in range. Wolfgang lashed out a left jab with the speed of a snake. Lee weaved but Wolfgang's massive fist caught him on the side of his head and sent him sprawling against the ropes. Wolfgang closed in fast for a right hook, but Lee was on the floor rolling. Then he was on his feet behind Wolfgang and dancing like a butterfly. I looked for a bruise, or a cut, but I couldn't see one.

Abbas looked down at me and smiled. "Round two," he said. "The Korean won't get to round three."

Lee was circling again and Wolfgang was cutting him off again, pressing him into the ropes. Abbas leaned down toward me, keeping his eyes on the fight. "Lee is using up energy, weaving and dancing, while Wolfgang has only to stand there, cut off his circling and hammer him with blows."

As he spoke, a front kick caught Lee on his arm. He dodged a second one, but Wolfgang followed up with a side kick that drove into his belly and hurled him against the ropes, making the wooden posts creak. He rolled and got to his feet, dancing away apparently unhurt. The crowd were shouting at him to dance, to dodge, to attack. I heard Abbas laugh quietly. He glanced at me and shook his head. "He can't take that kind of punishment indefinitely."

What he hadn't seen was that Lee had ridden the side kick. Wolfgang's foot had struck his cupped hands in front of his belly and thrown himself on the ropes. It had thrown him, but it hadn't penetrated; just as the punches had barely touched him. Wolfgang had delivered three good blows, and Lee was unhurt.

Wolfgang was looking fazed. I glanced at Abbas. He was frowning too. Wolfgang hurled himself at Lee in two furious spinning back kicks. He was fast and strong, but not fast enough. Lee ducked and danced and was miles away by the time Wolfgang was on his second kick. He landed looking for Lee. That was dangerous and they both knew it. Wolfgang was scowling, and now Lee was smiling. Wolfgang closed in again. He was more focused now, more concentrated, but also more careful. He started jabbing with his left, but Lee danced and dodged the punches easily. He dodged a couple of front and side kicks and then the gong went. Lee had done little but dance, and I got the idea he could dance all day. Wolfgang had expended a lot of energy, and now he was tired. The two went to their starting places and rested.

Abbas looked at me. "OK, he can dance and he can dodge, but that isn't enough. Wolfgang has the power. He will kill him."

I nodded and smiled. "Yeah, that's what Putin thought."

He arched an eyebrow at me, but didn't answer. Beyond him I saw Bob frown. After thirty seconds the gong rang for the second round. This time Lee walked to the center of the ring. Wolfgang approached him with caution, but then charged with a sudden, blistering roundhouse. If it had caught Lee it would have killed him, but it didn't. He crouched and let it skim over his head. As it passed he lashed out with his fingertips and hit Wolfgang in his calf muscle. Wolfgang didn't pause. He followed up with a spinning back kick, but by now Lee was on his left.

I didn't see the move. It was too fast, but there was a noise like a whip crack and Wolfgang was staggering sideways across the ring, holding his left shoulder. Lee was dancing and smiling. Wolfgang closed in again. His eyes were narrow and you could see his jaw muscle bouncing. If he hadn't known it before, now he knew he was fighting for his life. He threw three left jabs. On each one Lee dodged, and jabbed at Wolfgang's underarm with his fingertips. Wolfgang followed up with a right upper cut, but Lee wasn't there. He was on Wolfgang's left again, in the rider's stance, feet planted wide apart, knees bent. I reckon he punched three times, but it might have been four or five. He moved too fast to see, and his muscles were stretched taut like strings. He pounded into Wolfgang's shoulder, where he'd hit him before. Wolfgang let out a strange, strangled roar and staggered away, clutching at his shoulder again. Now his eyes were wide, on fire with rage and fear.

Lee was dancing again, relaxed, with his arms dangling by his side. I leaned over to Abbas and said, "Abbas, this is called death by a thousand cuts. It's an education. It teaches us that there are many kinds of power."

Maybe he didn't hear me. Maybe he was too engrossed in the fight, or maybe he believed that masters and gods had nothing to learn from mere heroes. Whatever the reason, he didn't respond.

Wolfgang's left arm was now hanging limp. He was going to have to rely on his right arm and his legs. They both knew that. And they both knew that, though Wolfgang was strong, each one of his legs weighed as much as Lee. Throwing them around was going to be tiring, especially for a man who was already half spent and in pain.

Wolfgang's instinct was to attack. He lunged in a powerful, surging side kick. It was verging on desperation. Lee lashed out with his fingertips again and struck at the calf muscle. Wolfgang followed up with a roundhouse. Lee dodged again and struck with his fingers, again at the calf. Wolfgang was beginning to limp. Now there was less rage in his eyes than fear. Lee stopped dancing. He stopped smiling. The seconds were counting down to the bell. He took two small, skipping steps, jumped and spun in the air with a speed that was not really human. Wolfgang could not have seen it. The back of his heel smashed into Wolfgang's temple and he crumpled like a broken toy. He lay on the mat, motionless. The crowd was silent.

With absolutely no expression on his face, Lee went and stood at Wolfgang's head. He carefully placed the blade of his right foot against the back of Wolfgang's neck, measured a couple of times and then, with a shriek like a seagull, and inhuman speed, he stamped. There was a crunch and Wolfgang's arms and legs jerked and twitched a few times. Then he lay still. Maybe his spirit was in Valhalla, the Hall of the Fallen.

Abbas did not look amused. I gave him a smile that might have been a little smug.

"Do gods pay their gambling debts, Abbas? Or do they just give out blessings?"

He spoke without looking at me.

"Believe me, Harry, I will pay you everything I owe you, but I will give you no blessings. Of that you may be sure."

"Good." I grinned. "Because I'd rather have a thousand bucks than a thousand blessings. What happens now?"

"Now?" He turned and looked down at me. "Now the Korean dies. If I say someone dies, Harry, they die." He turned and stared into the crowd. There was a kind of sick silence. I figured ninety-nine out of every hundred of these fools had never seen one man kill another, and they had just discovered it wasn't romantic and glorious. It was ugly and sickening.

Four guys were dragging Wolfgang's corpse away and Lee was sitting cross-legged, apparently meditating. Abbas's voice rang out:

"Olaf Olafsen, step into the ring. Step into the ring and let me see if you are capable of killing Jack Lee."

Olaf stood. At six-foot-six, slim, broad and athletic, he made Wolfgang look like a rhinoceros. He stepped easily into the ring, and studying his eyes I knew this guy had killed before, and enjoyed it.

TEN

THE GONG RANG AND OLAFSEN WAS THE FIRST TO THE center of the ring. He didn't do anything. He just stood there watching Lee circle around him. Lee was dancing again. He knew that, as with Wolfgang, he had less reach with his punches and kicks. Olafsen was a foot taller and could hit Lee while he was still out of range. So, as with Wolfgang, Lee had to dance to try to intercept his attacks and get in on the angles. But Olafsen didn't move. He just stood there and watched.

When he saw Olafsen wasn't going to make the first move he went for the death by a thousand cuts technique he'd used on Wolfgang. He danced into range and flicked a kick at Olafsen's shin. The kick found its target, but didn't seem to hurt. He danced a little more, ducking and diving, then spun under Olafsen's guard and gave him a powerful back kick to the knee. Olafsen's leg lifted, yielded and came back down. No pain. No damage.

Now he started to cut across Lee's path as Lee tried to dance around him. He was pressing him up closer to the ropes, forcing an attack out of him. Lee spun again, trying for a spinning back kick. This time he aimed a little higher, at the groin. I didn't see the kick. It was too fast. But when his foot made contact Olafsen was already on one knee with Lee's heel in his left hand, and his right forearm was crashing in to break Lee's knee. But Lee was too fast for that. He used Olafsen's hand as leverage and lashed out with his left heel, kicking Olafsen in the face and doing a back flip to land on his feet again. There was a collective gasp. Olafsen was staggering back. Lee didn't pause. He came at him again in a scissor kick that smashed his nose and drew blood. As he landed on the mat Lee was already flattening out for a spinning sweep which knocked Olafsen's feet from under him. He landed on his back with a huge thud. There were cries and shouts, and the gong went.

Olafsen got to his feet. Lee was doing a little victory dance, his feet and fists going so fast you couldn't see them. Olafsen ignored him and went to his corner.

Abbas was laughing. "Maybe I should change my prediction. You want to double the bet, Harry? Two thousand dollars says the Korean will kill the Viking."

I shook my head. "Olafsen is sizing Lee up. He has his measure now. He'll kill him in the next round."

"Always contrary and contradictory. Is this you, Harry? You need to go against the current and have the last word?"

"Not really, Abbas. I just know a lot about killing."

The gong went and Lee was in the middle of the ring, dancing, confident. I could see his eyes and they were on fire. I was sorry for him. He deserved to live.

Olafsen walked to the center of the ring and almost immediately started backing away. He was making his move, but Lee was too fired up by his early success to see it. Olafsen made a couple of long-range feints. He was fast and a couple of the blows hit their mark. They didn't hurt Lee, but they made it look like he was trying to. So Lee closed in. They exchanged a few more blows. Then, when he was about four feet from the ropes, Olafsen suddenly squared up to Lee and swung with a huge right hook. If he'd hit him it would have ripped his head off. But he didn't. Lee was much too fast.

He ducked and the hook went straight over his head. As he came up out of the crouch he inched forward with his left foot and slammed his right foot up in a powerful right front kick that caught Olafsen square in the solar plexus. Only it didn't. Because he'd brought his right arm out of the right hook down over his belly, and he supported it with his left palm. He'd known he was going to miss the punch, and he'd known exactly how Lee was going to react. He rode the kick. It lifted him off the tatami and threw him back six feet. Lee was roaring like a wild animal. All his muscles were corded all over his body as he sprang forward and rammed his fist into where Olafsen's face should have been.

Only Olafsen had landed on one knee and his face was three feet below where it should have been. Lee realized his mistake too late and Olafsen delivered a massive uppercut to his crotch. Lee staggered back a few steps and then fell to the ground on his back.

They thought it was over, but I knew they were wrong. Lee was finished, but Olafsen wasn't. He knew his job wasn't just to kill his opponent. He had to destroy him. He stood and walked over to where Lee was lying in agony. In one swift, violent movement he gripped Lee by the hair and dragged him over to the ropes. There he pulled him to his feet and leaned him on the ropes so he was facing out toward the crowd.

I couldn't look. He beat him for the last minute of the round. He beat him in the kidneys with blows from his feet and his fists that would have smashed concrete. He literally beat the life out of him, there, facing the crowd. And the crowd, infected with bloodlust, cheered and laughed and applauded. And that was the last thing Lee saw before he died. One hundred colleagues and companions, cheering his humiliation and his death.

Abbas turned in his throne and regarded me for a long moment. It was the look of a god who has twice been shown to be wrong by a mere mortal.

"You know a lot about death, Harry. I think perhaps it is time for you to become a real master. A master is one who has died and been reborn. Go, see if there is anything you can teach Olaf."

I nodded slowly to him. I felt Anna's small, cold hand on my arm. I ignored her and stood, stripped off my jacket and shirt and stepped into the ring. I didn't bow to Abbas. I didn't feel like it. I walked to the center of the tatami and jerked my chin at Olaf.

"You rested or you need a little longer?"

His eyes flicked over me, calibrating me. "I am rested."

The gong sounded and he walked toward me without hesitation. He didn't think. He didn't need to. He was the best living fighter I had ever seen. He caught me by surprise and moved too fast for the eye to see. He struck me backhanded and knocked me sprawling to the ground. I scrambled to my feet and tried to dodge to one side, but he was there ahead of me, reading my movements. He struck me again and I went down again.

My head was reeling, but I knew I had to keep moving and keep thinking. If I paused I died, and as I clambered to my feet, staggering backwards away from him, I was thinking that this was a show. He was here as a demonstration of Abbas's power. Just as he had destroyed Lee in the name of Abbas, now he would aim to string out my death, make it last.

So I had a chance.

I skipped round, backing up almost to the ropes, so I had my back to where I'd been sitting. I sneered at him, 'That the best you've got? What's next? You gonna hit me with your handbag, or get your mom to come and help you?' He cocked his head on one side, a little surprised. I knew what was coming, and I knew I had to time it exactly right. He shifted his weight and lunged at me in a side kick. I hunkered down and leaned to my right, opening my belt buckle as I did so. And as his foot plowed through the gap in the ropes, I scrambling to my feet, pulling my belt loose as I ran. By that time he had disengaged his foot and was already after me. I felt his hand grab my neck, then his other hand had me by the seat of my pants. I was in the air and he hurled me against the corner post of the ring. Shards of pain stabbed into my lungs and I felt the warm blood running down my back and my arm as I rolled on the mat.

He was on me again. He grabbed me by my hair, wrenched me to my feet and threw me across the mat again. I focused on rolling, ignored the pain, and came up on one knee.

I was in the middle of the ring now. I was holding the belt by the end of the strap, with the buckle hanging loose, out of sight behind my leg. Olaf charged me. He was expecting me to get to my feet, maybe try to run; but he knew he'd be too fast for me and he was planning a side kick or a front kick. But I'd made a career out of not doing what people expected me to do, and just as he launched into his kick I fell. I fell on my back and I looped my belt around his ankle and pulled. He was two hundred and fifty pounds of charging muscle and he fell like a ton weight, slamming his head on the hard ground.

I was on my feet, swinging the belt over my head. He was on his hands and knees, struggling to his feet, and I let him have it with the buckle across his face five or six times. Maybe that was a mistake. It didn't stop him but it made him real mad. I figured I was going to die anyway, so I might as well have the satisfaction of drawing blood.

He moved with the speed of a viper. He was off his knees and at me before I saw him shift. He took my shoulder and spun me, and as I spun he hooked my ankle and I was sprawling on my face. Then he had me by the hair and up on all fours. He came down behind me, pinning me with his thighs. One of his massive hands went over my face, the other grabbed the back of my head, and I knew what he was going to do. He was going to end it by breaking my neck.

And in that moment I knew that I wasn't going to let him do that. There was a fire in my belly and a wild rage that said I wasn't ready to die yet. I fought back, but I knew I couldn't resist his strength. I also knew that if you think about your neck when someone is trying to break it, you're going to die. You have to think about the other guy, and his weak spots, and what weapons you can use.

I felt the belt buckle in my hand and thumbed out the

prong. I could feel Olaf's head right on top of mine, breathing hard with the effort. I controlled my movement. I had to judge it just right, and I did. I rammed the prong of the buckle hard into his right eye. I felt the gush of warm liquid on my hand. His scream was like the scream of a dinosaur, yet somehow pathetic. He was on his feet, staggering back, away from me, toward the ropes, where a wooden post stood. This time I didn't think. I was on my feet, driven by rage and hatred. I ran at him, leapt into a scissor kick and smashed his face with my right heel. All two hundred and fifty pounds of him crashed back against the post. The post gave and came loose, pulling the ropes down with it.

I lunged at him and kicked him again, first in the ribs and then again, in the head. I was in the raging frenzy that grips a man on the very brink of death. I kicked and stamped at his head, at his neck, at any vulnerable spot I could find. He bellowed and yelled a couple of times, then sagged. I roared, grabbed the post with both hands and ripped it from the ground. The ropes came free and I raised it above my head and rammed it down, plunging it through his ribs and into his heart. He made a horrific sound in his throat and his mouth. His arms and legs twitched and jerked, and he lay still.

I turned, trembling, and looked up at Abbas under my brows. He was watching me carefully. Maybe he knew in that moment that I was coming for him. I had just killed a man who had done nothing to me except obey the mindless orders of this narcissistic clown, and in that moment I knew beyond any doubt that I would kill Abbas Magomadov.

I raised my voice and was surprised to hear that it was steady and firm.

"Is there anybody else you want me to kill today, Abbas?"

He stood and pointed at me, addressing the silent crowd.

"This is a mighty warrior, a great hero like those of old. This man has died, and found the truth of his immortality. This man I will have close to my heart, as my guardian in this world." He turned to Anna. "Take him inside, have the women bathe him and anoint him, feed him and give him wine."

Suddenly I'd had enough. I turned and left the ring and made my way along the dirt road toward the big house. I felt sick at what I had just done. I told myself I had been fighting for my life, it had been self-defense, and that Olaf himself had been no stranger to killing. But it made no difference, because inside I knew that I had been here, available for the combat, because I had chosen to come here on a mission of death. Somebody had said it, some asshole self-help guru—you get more of what you focus on.

I heard feet running behind me and ignored them, with a growing sense of anger burning in my belly. A small hand gripped my arm and I turned. Anna was there, staring up at me. For once there was something like emotion in her eyes, but right then I was too mad to care.

"What? God told you to take me and anoint me, and hand me over to his damned harem, and you have to obey?"

"Yes."

"I can manage fine on my own, and a shower and a whiskey will do just fine."

I turned to walk away but she tugged on my arm again.

"Wait!"

"What?" I snarled the word and saw her frown.

"Why are you angry with me?"

I struggled to find an answer. I started, "Because..." but couldn't continue. Instead I said, "This is not..." but trailed off again. "It's not you. Forget it."

I walked away, but her voice, falling away behind me, said, "I can't."

I stopped and turned back. "Why? Because God told you not to?"

"No. Because I don't want you to be angry at me. I did do nothing. I spoke to the Master good things about you."

This was another face to Anna, and it was unexpected. If you're a newcomer, some guy off the street, you get the blunt, harsh Russian treatment. But show you're a mean bastard and she becomes sweet and submissive. That was why she adored Abbas. I felt a sudden surge of nausea, but also of pity for her. She was lost in a dark storm and had nothing to hold on to but a sinking ship.

"Come on," I said, "you can fix me a drink, but I don't want to be anointed and I don't want Abbas's damned harem."

ELEVEN

SHE FOLLOWED ME TO MY ROOM AND FIXED US A COUPLE of drinks while I showered. I stood under the powerful stream of hot water and tried to think. One thing was clear above all others. I needed to talk to the brigadier and he needed to know what was going on here. While I was toweling myself dry she sat on the bed watching me, and finally said, "You must stop your angry behavior. Or the master will kill you. He has killed many men."

I dropped the towel on the bathroom floor and pulled on my jeans. I considered her a moment before doing up my belt.

"This is not what I was looking for, Anna. Is this what you want?"

"It's what the Master wants. This is the Church of Nergal. He is the god of war."

"Yeah, I know, but the idea is, after you've had a life of war and killing, you then find peace..."

She was shaking her head and I trailed off.

"Death and war never stop, Harry. It is the cycle, round and round. Some men are born to kill, like you, like the Master."

"Yeah?" I grabbed my shirt and pulled it on. "I didn't see him do much killing today. It seems to me he had other people do it for him."

She shrugged. "He is the Master."

"Yeah, right. I need to talk to him in private. Can you arrange that?"

"Maybe."

"Good. Do it. Also," I paused, thinking fast, my mind racing, "I need to go to Hermosillo. Can you arrange a car?"

She shook her head, frowning. "You cannot go to Hermosillo."

"What do you mean, I can't go to Hermosillo?"

"It is not permitted."

I sighed, finding it ever harder to suppress my anger. "OK, fine. What about vehicles? Where are they kept?"

Her frown turned from concern to distress. "Why? What do you intend to do? You are out of control, Harry. You must stop."

I forced a laugh. "Relax, will you. I don't plan to do anything. I'm going to meet up with Abbas, ask him for permission to drive over to Hermosillo, borrow a car and drive there and back. No big deal."

"Harry," she stepped up close and grabbed the open collar of my shirt, "Harry, he will not let you go. Please don't do anything crazy. You know I will have to pay if you do—even if you just ask —because I brought you here. Nobody is allowed to leave, in case..."

She trailed off.

"In case what?"

She hesitated. "He does not want anyone to know where we are. That is why your cell phone was removed. We must not make contact with anyone until the Master says it is OK."

"Anna, will you relax? I am not going to do anything crazy, I am not going to contact anyone or tell them where we are, and I sure as hell am not going to put you at risk. I just want to know where the vehicles are kept. I'll borrow it and no one will even know I've gone. Will you tell me, or do I have to go snooping around to find them?"

"*Harry!* Please stop!"

"Fine!" I played mad and pulled away from her. "Don't tell me. That's cool. I'll go find someone who is willing to talk to me. Maybe one of those Japanese girls, or—"

She was shaking her head. "No, Harry. They will all report back to the Master."

"I'll have to take my chances."

"You will take chances with my life. If you take a vehicle they will torture me and kill me for putting the church at risk by bringing you here. Harry, *please!*"

I walked up to her and held her face in my hands. "Tell me where the vehicles are kept and I will make sure no harm comes to you. Refuse to help me and I'll have no choice but to put you at risk. You decide."

She closed her eyes. "The vehicles are all kept in the garage, the old stables in back of this building."

"What vehicles?"

"Two Land Rover, a Range Rover, a couple of Wranglers. But Harry, please, they will kill me..."

"Relax, will you?"

"What do you need in Hermosillo? You have everything you need right here. You have changed. First you were on a spiritual quest, now this crazy behavior. What is going on with you?"

My mind was spinning, careening back and forth, searching for some kind of story that would make any kind of sense. I spoke without thinking. "My mother," I said at last.

She frowned the frown of the deeply confused. "Your *mother?*"

"What? Guys like me can't have mothers?"

"But..."

"She has cancer, she hasn't long to live, I told her I'd call her."

She shook her head again. It was a small, helpless gesture. "You cannot have these attachments."

I injected real bitterness into my voice. "Yeah, will pretty soon I won't have. All I want to do is say goodbye to the woman who gave me life. Is that such a bad thing?" I went and stared out of the window. "You know, I hear a lot of talk about freedom and the individualism of the warrior," I turned back to face her, "but all I see is a bunch of slaves being told what they can and cannot do. You wonder why I've changed? Well that is a good part of the reason, right there."

"You are a subversive," she said in a small voice.

"Yeah, that's what warriors are. Soldiers obey orders and get killed on the front line, warriors go behind the lines and subvert." She didn't say anything and I knew I was in trouble. "You're going to report me to Abbas, aren't you?"

"No,"

"You're going to tell him I want to go and talk to my mother."

"No."

"You're going to humiliate me in front of everyone, a mother's boy who can't shake free of his mother's bonds."

"Harry, stop it. I am not going to do that. I will arrange a meeting for you. I know you are a man of your word. All I ask is that you tell him about your mother, that she is dying and you need to say goodbye. I know he will understand that."

"You'll do that for me?"

"Yes, Harry. But if I can give you some advice, tell him you need also to talk to your bank about arranging the second transfer."

It was simple. I should have thought of that. I smiled. "You're cute. I'll do that."

She gave me a kiss that was surprisingly warm and left the room. I had time to pull on my boots and a shirt before there was a knock at the door. I opened it and found Bohdan Fedorko, aka Bob, looking uncertain.

"Hello, Bob, what can I do for you?"

"I can come inside?"

"Sure." I stepped back and he moved in, glancing over his shoulder. "Is three a problem?"

He reached the middle of the floor before he stopped and turned to face me. I waited while he chewed his lip. Finally he said, "Why are you here?"

"You collected me and brought me here, remember?"

He shook his head. "I collected you and brought you here, yes, but why? Because you pay a big sum of money to the church." He shrugged. "So it is normal Ab—the Master will want to meet you."

"What are you getting at?"

"You are a very dangerous man."

"Yeah. What are you driving at, Bobby. Get to the point."

"You have a drink? I am nervous."

I poured him a drink and pointed at a chair beside a table. "Take a seat. What's making you nervous?"

He sat, took the drink, looked at it a moment like his life would change if he drank it, and took a hefty swig. After he'd smacked his lips and squeezed his eyes he said, "You. You make me nervous."

I pulled up a chair and sat opposite him. I remembered the brigadier telling me once that when people keep giving you vague answers you have to close your questions.

"What is it about me," I said very deliberately, "that makes you nervous?"

He pushed his glass toward me, held my eye a moment and said, "I think you are here to kill the Master."

I made a face that told him I was bored, leaned back in my chair and sighed.

"Bob, go tell Abbas I am not here to kill him, I am here to learn from him, but if he wants to get his two hundred and fifty grand he had better up his damned game. Because so far I am less than impressed."

"What are you talking about?"

"Come on, Bob! What are we, in kindergarten? He didn't like my lack of respect this morning, he's seen I have skills and now he's worried one of his enemies has sent me to get him. So he sends you along with this chicken shit ploy..."

I trailed off because he was shaking his head. He made it look urgent.

"No," he said, "No, no no. Stop, please. In the first place—" He stopped and pointed his finger at me. "You say it yourself. He is too smart to do something stupid like that. This is me, I come because you make me nervous. You are like a crazy man, going around, bam! Bam! Bam!"

I made that face you make when you're sixteen and your girl-friend asks you why you love her. "Listen, I made a mistake. I saw the website, and the website is cool. If this outfit was like the website, that would be great. But this is a joke, Bob." I sat forward and leaned my elbows on the table. "I have trained and worked with the best, and I have seen too much death, year after year. I don't know how many men I have killed, and the worst thing, Bob, I have forgotten *why* I killed them. My soul is not going to hell. My soul is already in hell, and I was looking for a real master to show me how to get out. All I have found is some crazy son of a bitch who wants to keep on killing. That's not what I signed up for."

He stared at me for a long moment. I stood up and grabbed his glass.

"Bob, listen, I know Abbas sent you to find out what I'm about. It's cool. Don't worry about it. I'm going to talk to him myself. I know I'm going to have to pay..."

But he was shaking his head again. "Stop saying that. I risk my life to come here and talk to you. The Master did not send me."

"You want to give me one good reason why I should believe you?"

He drew breath, hesitated then shook his head.

"What you ask is impossible. I am devoted to the Master, and to the Church of Nergal, but he did not send me. I came myself because I want to know why you are here. I know you are not who you say you are. You have some purpose," he hesitated again, then said, "I must say no more."

I stepped in front of the door, blocking the exit, and crossed my arms.

"You are devoted to Abbas, you are devoted to the Church of Nergal, you think I am here on a mission to kill Abbas, but instead of telling him, you come here—not to kill me, not to confront me, not with Abbas's personal guard. No, you come alone, as though your intention was to help me."

His eyes searched mine and he swallowed hard. I waited, but his throat just kept swallowing, like he was swallowing all the words he wanted to say.

"Where is Abbas now?"

"Why? What are you going to do?"

"Where is he? How do I find him?"

"What are you going to tell him about me?"

"Nothing. I'm not in a position to rock any boats, Bob. I've upset him enough as it is. I just want to talk to him."

"What about?"

"None of your damned business."

"Tell me! You don't know what is going on here! You don't know how dangerous is this situation! Stop being a fool! Tell me!"

I looked at him hard. He was either a damned good actor, or he was in serious trouble and looking for help.

"All right, I want to talk to him about my mother."

"*What?*"

"Sure." I took a couple of steps closer to him. "She's sick. She's dying. I need to go to Hermosillo to call her to say goodbye. I also need to make arrangements to have a quarter of a million backs transferred to his account."

"This is a fantastically stupid idea. He will never believe it and he will have you killed."

I felt like telling him it was the best I could do thinking on my feet with zero options. He must have seen it in my face because he sighed and ran his hands through his hair.

"What is your real reason for going to Hermosillo?" I was in the same situation I had been in with Anna. Not a single, credible reason came to my mind. He went on, "This story about your mother, it is stupid. Have you told anybody else?" One look at my eyes told him I had. He sagged, threw his head back and covered his face. "*O Bozhe!* Who did you tell? Anna?" Again, my face said I had. He turned away, literally gripping his hair with his hands. "*Yob tvoyu mat'! Auka khuylo!* I thought you were smart!"

"Cut it out, will you!"

He turned to face me. "Cut it out? Cut it out is what they are going to do with your living, fucking heart before they eat it raw! Right after Anna tells him what you plan to do!"

"So why do you care?"

He hesitated for just a second, then wagged his finger in the negative.

"No, we share, we share. No one-way deal. Is like your mother being sick. Bullshit explanation. So my bullshit explanation is when I met you I like you. I think you are an asshole and I want help you before you fuck up completely and get killed. What did you tell her?"

"I told her to fix up a meeting with Abbas. When I see him I'll tell him I need to go to Hermosillo, to talk to my mother and arrange the second transfer. For that I'll need a car."

"That simple."

"Why make it complicated. It's the truth." I shrugged. "I could have him send somebody with me. You could offer, or Anna."

"*Auka khuylo!* You trust that woman? You love her or something? You cannot see what she is?"

"I don't love her, Bob. I see what she is. Will you relax a little? I need to go to Hermosillo. I have to work with what I've got."

He ran his hands through his hair again and muttered what I was pretty sure were obscenities. When he was done he said, "OK, I will talk with the Master, try to limit damage that Anna will have caused. I will convince him have meeting with you. Now she has told him, we have no choice. You must continue with bullshit about mother, but make emphasis on the money. I will suggest I go with you."

I nodded and he pushed past me to the door. There he paused and I told him, "Thanks."

To which he replied, "*Auka khuylo!*" and left.

TWELVE

I DIDN'T HAVE TO WAIT LONG. FIFTEEN MINUTES LATER there was a rap at the door. Before I could answer it, it opened and a guy in fatigues stepped in with an automatic rifle over his shoulder. He was tall and thick, like the result of a night of drunken passion between a lonely gorilla and a sow who'd been stood up by her date.

"You come with me. The Master will see you."

I looked past him into the corridor. There were two more pigrillas outside. I stepped up close to him and looked into his eyes, seeking a glimmer of consciousness. There wasn't one. I spoke so quiet it was almost a whisper.

"Next time you knock at my door, you wait till I say come in, or I will tear out your intestines and lynch you with them."

There might have been a tiny frown, but all he said was, "Come," and marched out of the room.

I followed him to the left along the long, wooden corridor, down a flight of steps and along another passage to a set of large, double doors at the end. There were two guards outside it, also in fatigues and holding assault rifles. The pigrilla hammered on the door, waited till a voice called, "Come!" and opened the door.

He turned to me and pointed, "Go in."

I went in. The walls were wood paneled and lined with book-cases. A large log fire burned on a brick pedestal in the middle of the room, where a copper flue caught the smoke and carried it up through the rafters of an A-frame ceiling. The floor was covered in an eclectic scattering of Persian rugs and animal skins. At the far end of the room there was a huge, plate-glass window with an uninterrupted view of sand dunes and the Gulf of California. A nest of worn leather chairs and a sofa stood close to the fire, flanked by heavy wooden lamp tables with big, fat lamps. Abbas was sitting at his desk reading, but looked up and stood as I came in. He pointed at the nest of chairs and made his way there, speaking as he went.

"I think it's time we talked, Harry. Don't you? Sit down." He lowered himself into a chair and I sat opposite him. "Let me start," he said, "so you know where we stand. Then I hand over to you." He waited a moment. I didn't say anything so he went on. "I like you." He spread his hands and shrugged. "You are a danger to me in many ways, to my authority, to my reputation... We talk about that later. But still, though you are a risk, I like you. You know why I like you?"

I assumed it was a rhetorical question so I didn't say anything again. He watched me a moment and nodded.

"People do not belong in categories, Harry," he shook his head and told me, in case I didn't know what categories were, "black, white, man, woman, ignorant, educated..."

"I know what categories are."

"People do not belong to categories. People *hide* in categories, so they don't have to take the responsibility of being individuals. But you, you are like me. You do not seek a category where you can hide. You are a unique, individualistic, predatory son of a bitch."

"What's your point?"

"My point is this: that there is a place here for you. I have plans and I can use the help and collaboration of a man like you.

We can make insane amounts of money, and we can accrue the kind of power that makes governments sit up and pay attention."

"You're fantasizing."

"Oh, for sure, but one of the strengths of a man who knows who and what he is, is that he can fantasize, and then he can make his fantasy real. Bush, Obama, Trump, Biden—" He spat elaborately and with skill into the fire. "This guys come to 'power,'" he laughed and made the little speech marks with his fingers, "because the society which they hide in not only allowed them to become president, it *required* them to become president. But Hitler? George Washington? Napoleon? These men created a world, a new reality, in which they were like gods. *That* is real, creative power. It is what I saw in the mountains, it is the illumination I had, and it is what I am doing. I am creating a new reality, in which I am god."

"It sounds like hell. What makes you think I want to be a part of that?"

He sat forward with his elbows on his knees. "I don't think that, Harry. I suspect that like me, you believe it is better to rule in hell than to serve in paradise. So I want to know what you want and why you are here. I am telling you I like you, I respect your power and I am willing to make room for you. Now I want you to tell me, what are you looking for in my church?"

"I already told you—"

"So!" he interrupted me. "I have no problem killing you." He laughed. "Nobody gets out of here alive. I have killed people I like many times. Now I tell you how this works. You worry me, you are a threat to me, you are a problem, I talk to you, we reach an understanding and we are good. No problem." He paused, spread his hands, shrugged, pulled down the corners of his mouth. It was all very expressive. "But you *don't* talk to me, we *don't* reach an understanding, well, then, I kill you and the problem goes away. To live, we must understand each other." He jerked his chin at me. "What were you saying?"

I didn't speak for a moment. I was beginning to feel trapped and I was looking for a way out. "Did Anna speak to you?"

"Anna speaks to me all the time."

"About going to Hermosillo."

He screwed up his face and gestured at me with an open hand. "You see? This is what I don't like. Evasive. I invite you to communicate and reach a mutual understanding, and what do you do? You become evasive."

"I'm not being evasive, Abbas. I need to know. Did Anna talk to you about—"

"Yeah, yeah. She talked about it, and Bohdan too. You want to go to Hermosillo, some bullshit about your mother and the bank and blah, blah, blah. You use my inner circle to try to manipulate me. You are close to death, Harry, and you are playing it all wrong. You need to start talking to me. Make me trust you."

I took a deep breath. The son of a bitch was right. Too often, I told myself, I found myself agreeing with the stuff he said.

"OK." I nodded slowly a couple of times. "The truth. My mother died a long time ago. I needed an excuse and that was the first thing that came into my mind when I was talking to Anna."

"That is not important. You used what was available. The question is, Why do you want to go to Hermosillo?"

"I do need to make the trans—"

He wagged his finger in the negative. "Any second now, Harry, I will suddenly lose my patience and call in the boys. You might kill one or two, I don't doubt it. You might kill me. I don't care. But you will die and it will be the end of your story. Now, again, why do you want to go to Hermosillo?"

He had me in a corner and I could not see a way out. I arched an eyebrow at him and sighed at the floor. "Let me finish my answer, will you?" I made a question with my face and showed it to him. He waited so I said, "The truth. I work for the CIA Special Activities Center. They want you for the war crimes in Chechnya, when you were with the 141st Special Motorized Regiment, the Kadyrovitsy. The massacre at Novye-Yurt, amongst others."

He knit his brows. "They think I am dead."

"Wrong. They picked up your trail in Turkey. It took time but they followed it first to Australia, where you almost pulled it off with the dead hiker, and then to San Francisco. I found your body in Manzanilla Avenue. You almost had us fooled, but you used a similar technique in Oz—the mutilation of a body. Only this time you went a little further." I pointed at his hand. "Trouble is, your double, though he was very like you, his hands were not identical and the ME detected the discrepancy. He was a thorough man and ran DNA tests on various part of the body besides the hand. He found the hand belonged to somebody else. It was a subtle play, Abbas, but you wasted a perfectly good hand."

He looked away at the big, plate-glass window. He half whispered, "*Vot eto pizdets!* So you are here hunting me?" I nodded. "Why are you telling me so easy?" He narrowed his eyes. "A man like you. It does not make sense."

"It makes perfect sense, believe me. Now I need you to listen very carefully, and think, because in a minute you are going to get mad."

"Tell me..."

"If you were in my position, what would you prefer, to work for the CIA, or have a part of this?" I indicated the camp as a whole with my finger. He arched an eyebrow and I nodded. "Yeah, you're right. I'd rather rule in hell. Now, understand this, Abbas. The hundred grand I paid you? It's a ghost. It looks like it's in your account, but the moment they pull the plug it vanished."

"Son of a whore."

"Stay with me, Abbas. I figure you're in Mexico because you want to move in on one of the cartels. I've seen the quality of your men. They're OK, they can be a lot better, but they're OK. I figure you might even pull it off, with the right help. But I also figure the minute you realize the money is a ghost, I am dead." I paused and took another deep breath. "So, I needed to go to Hermosillo for exactly the reason I told you, to make the transfer of two hundred and fifty thousand dollars to your account." I paused. "But there was more to it than that."

"What?"

"I wasn't going to Hermosillo. I was going to Mexico City."

"You better start talking straight, Harry. I am losing my patience."

"Do you think the CIA would be willing to pay you three hundred and fifty thousand dollars? You think they'd be happy to leave you the hundred they'd already paid, and pay you another two fifty on top? You think they'd do that?"

He cautiously shook his head, wondering where I was going.

"Well, you'd be wrong, Abbas. The CIA has all the moral conscience of a flesh-eating bacterium. The CIA helped to set up the Sinaloa Cartel in the first place, and even provided them with Panama as a banking haven where they could do deals undisturbed, But Sinaloa has become a problem now because they have become too powerful. They have penetrated law enforcement, the judiciary and even Congress. Now the US pumps money into Mexico to try to suppress Sinaloa, while the Mexican government siphons off the money into private accounts, does nothing and asks for more."

"So...?"

"So it seems to me that suddenly you and the CIA have a common interest. How about if I gave the CIA an alternative to Sinaloa? How about if the CIA not only paid you three hundred and fifty grand, but also funnelled the money they still make out of Sinaloa into the Church of Nergal, so you could break the back of the cartels and take over the coke and heroin trade? We are not talking about hundreds of thousands anymore, Abbas. We are now talking about thousands of millions. And *that* is why I needed to go to Mexico City, to talk to the CIA attaché at the embassy."

"You expect me to believe that?" He said it, but he said it without much conviction.

"You got a better explanation? Why do *you* think I wanted to go to Hermosillo?"

"To escape."

I laughed out loud. "Listen, Abbas, I am a professional. And I am really good at what I do. I am an expert in desert guerrilla warfare. You think if I wanted to escape, I would inform Anna and Bob, and then come and tell you about it? I do not want to escape. If I wanted to, believe me, I'd be gone by now. Try again."

"You really think the CIA—?"

"Come on, Abbas! It's what the CIA has been doing since it was created. They set up an insurgent, destabilizing organization, and when they get out of hand they destroy them: Iran, Afghanistan, Iraq. Trouble is they lost control of Sinaloa."

"They did the same in the Russian Commonwealth, after the Soviet Collapse."

I shrugged and nodded. "Think it through. We tracked you to San Francisco from Australia. How long do you think it will take them to figure out where we are now? And what do you think they'll do—what would you do—when they find you have what is basically a military base in the desert where you hold fights to the death? They will see you as a potential terrorist organization, mount a joint operation with the Mexicans, kill everybody here and claim it was a Waco, Jonestown set up—and they will probably claim they recovered six tons of coke and heroin for good measure. I'll be a hero and you'll be dead."

He grunted.

"But now figure," I went on, "if their undercover agent comes back to them and says, 'Hold your horses, I figure we have an opportunity here to bring down Sinaloa.'" I shrugged and gave a small laugh. "Hell, this is what the CIA does. This is their stock in trade."

He stood and looked into the fire for a while, then wandered over to the window and stood looking out at the ocean about a mile away. I said:

"You don't trust me. That is logical. I wouldn't trust me. But the answer is simple. Send a couple of your men with me. Anna adores you, literally, and so does Bob. Send them too if you want to. I'll arrange a meeting at the embassy—"

"How do I know you won't simply inform on me?"

I raised my voice like he was getting on my nerves. "Because they already know you're here, Abbas! And if they don't, they will do in a few days, or a week. They are watching you from space, for crying out loud! I joined the church, Bob picked me up from the hotel and I went off the radar. Where do you think they'll look for me? In Canada? The most law-abiding country on the continent? Or Mexico?"

He chewed his lip and I sighed. "I'll wear a wire. You can listen in on the conversation. And I guarantee, Abbas, when I get back, we will be arranging a celebratory feast, because you will have become a billionaire, and you will be planning the conquest of Mexico."

He closed his eyes, frowning hard. "Your original purpose in coming here..."

"I had no original purpose in coming here, Abbas! Think it through, will you? *You* brought me here! I followed you to San Francisco and joined the church because I was hunting for you— *in San Francisco!* It was you who brought me here, and when I saw the setup you had here, it changed everything. And now I am on the clock. Because when they see I have vanished, they are going to start looking for me. They will find me and they will come after me, and they will come after you. Me, because I am a valuable asset. You, because they want to kill you."

I watched his face and saw that somehow it made sense to him. He nodded a few times. "Everything changed when you realized I had this camp."

"Yes."

"Before you wanted to kill me. Now you want to use me."

"That's politics."

He stared me straight in the eye. "Whoever wields the most violence, is the most valuable."

"That is your philosophy and mine, Abbas. You have become a desirable commodity. You are achieving what you want, a lot faster than you expected."

He nodded. "All right. You go tonight. Anna stays here with me. If you betray me she will be punished because she brought you to me. I will choose two men and Bohdan will accompany you. You will wear a wire at your meeting."

I nodded and gave something like a smile. "You made the right choice."

THIRTEEN

THE TRIP TO MEXICO CITY WAS OVER A THOUSAND miles, some twenty hours by car through some of the most dangerous territory in the Americas. So instead of driving we took the plane, which was just two hours of moderate luxury instead. We departed early next morning and landed at the Adolfo Lopez Mateos Airport at ten thirty AM. From there it was an hour's drive through the mountains to the Sheraton, on the Paseo de la Reforma Avenue, in the heart of Mexico City, just a hundred yards from the embassy.

We managed to get four rooms next to each other, with Bob next to me and Ernesto and the pigrilla, whose name turned out to be Primitivo—seriously—had a room either side of us. After we had checked in we assembled in my room and, with Ernesto standing by the door and Primitivo the pigrilla standing by the balcony, Bob handed me my cell and sat on the bed to watch me.

"Call your contact at the embassy, Harry, and arrange the meeting. Put it on speakerphone, please."

"Don't try to organize me, Bob. I have to follow Company operating procedure. If I put it on speaker they'll notice, trace the call and have the place crawling with cops before you can say Nergal."

I called the brigadier and when he answered I said, "Good morning, this is Officer Harry Bauer, I need to talk to the liaison officer at the embassy in Mexico City."

There was a fractional pause, then, "Good morning, Officer Bauer. I take it you are an officer in the Central Intelligence Agency."

"That is correct."

"Can you confirm whether this conversation is being overheard by people outside the Agency?"

"It is not."

"Can you tell me what you need to talk to the liaison officer about?"

"In broad terms, but I would rather keep it on a need-to-know basis. I was detailed to execute a termination. It now seems that perhaps the organization to which the target was attached may have paramilitary potential which could be of use in bringing down cartels such as Sinaloa. That is all I am prepared to say over the telephone. I need a debriefing and further instructions."

"I'll get back to you in the next hour."

I hung up and spread my hands. "They'll get back to me in the next hour."

As it was he got back to me twenty minutes later.

"Yeah."

"Can you confirm that the line is secure and you are not being overheard?"

"Up to a point, yeah."

"You have a meeting at the embassy with the liaison officer at two o'clock this afternoon. Your case officer will be present by video link."

"Thank you, sir. I'll be there."

He hung up and I smiled at Bob. "Two o'clock at the embassy."

"You think they'll buy it?"

"Buy it? Buy what? It's not a question of buying it, Bob. This is a genuine recommendation from an officer to the Agency. The

Church of Nergal could genuinely have a powerful, positive impact and help to bring down the cartels. If we get rich in the process, what's the harm?"

"But you came to the Church to kill the Master."

"Yeah, and isn't that what you're all about, Bob? Aren't you in this damned setup to learn to rise above life and death, and be free? Yeah, I came as a killer, just as Abbas arrived as a killer at Novye-Yurt and slaughtered ten thousand people, men women and children—all except the girls who were given as gifts into slavery. Just as his regiment was deployed in Ukraine to murder and terrorize innocent people because they wanted independence. Yeah, I came to kill him, but I stayed to help him. So quit griping."

His face was impassive, impossible to read. But something told me if Primitivo the pigrilla and his simian friend hadn't been there, he might have had something to say.

We had a lunch of burgers and beer sent up and when we'd finished Bob provided me with a watch which doubled as a listening device. It functioned as a transmitter and also had recording capabilities. It made me wonder who was supplying his gear. As I put it on I told him, "Transmitting from inside the embassy is a bad idea. Not only will it be scrambled, they'll detect it and trace it within seconds. We leave the transmit function off. I'll record it and transmit it when I leave."

"The arrangement was you would transmit live during the meeting!"

"The arrangement was stupid."

He stood, staring at me hard. "Then why did you agree to it?"

"Because it was the only way to get Abbas onboard. It had to be on his terms and you know it. Now what do you want me to do, phone up and tell them my kidnappers won't let me go? Or maybe just not show up and have the CIA and the CNI scouring the country for us? How long do you think it would take them to find the base in Baja? Now, do you want to put your panties back on and show some professionalism and intelligence?"

"Take it easy, Harry."

"So stop wasting my time. It's one thirty. I'll see you in an hour or two."

I pulled on my jacket and they all watched me leave with varying expressions of dislike. That was OK. They weren't on my Christmas card list either.

I took the stairs down instead of the elevator and spent five minutes inspecting the newspapers in the lobby. I didn't see anybody I didn't like, so I stepped out into the street and turned right, away from the embassy. Nobody followed me. I turned right again, into the broad, bustling Eje 2, and then took another sharp right into the Rio Volga, a narrow back street that allowed me to approach the embassy along the Rio Danubio practically to the front door. I was alone all the way.

When I got inside there was a guy in a suit waiting for me. I saw him glance at a picture on his phone before he approached me.

"Are you Mr. Bauer?"

"Yeah."

"Please come with me."

He fast-tracked me through security and led me up some stairs to a set of elevators you don't get to see from the lobby. We didn't speak as we went up, or as we stepped out on the fifth floor and he showed me down a broad corridor to a nondescript door right at the end. There he knocked, leaned inside and murmured, "Mr. Harry Bauer..."

I heard a woman's voice, quiet but brisk, and my silent guide retracted his head and smiled at me. "Would you care to...?" He gestured at the open door but left it up to me to imagine his meaning.

I went inside and found a young man behind a desk typing into a computer. Behind him and to his left was a walnut door. He smiled at me and said, "Mr. Bauer? Major Sandy Silverman is expecting you, go right on in."

He pointed at the door. As I approached it buzzed and swung

open. I pushed through into an office that was more about work than status. The carpet was blue, most of the furniture was mahogany, there were a couple of leather armchairs and a tray of drinks on a shelf on the bookcase, but the focal point was the large, oak desk which was littered with files and well-thumbed books with markers in them. Behind the desk was the Stars and Stripes, a portrait of the president, a big, brown leather chair and a woman in her mid-fifties with chestnut hair, olive skin and a pair of eyes that could perform microsurgery on a gnat.

There was a laptop on the desk turned so that we could both see the screen. On that screen I could see the brigadier leafing through papers. I smiled and said, "Major."

She stood. "Mr. Bauer, may I call you Harry? Call me Sandy." We shook hands and she gestured to the chair on my side of her desk. I saw the brigadier look up but ignored him. As I sat I lifted the wire on her phone and showed it to her, then pointed to my watch as I said, "It's good of you to see me at such short notice. I imagine you have been in touch with Langley." I nodded as I said it.

She leaned back in her chair, watching me. "You bet."

"As you know I am with Special Activities. I am not sure how much they told you, but I was tasked with executing a target in San Francisco. The target is a Chechen war criminal named Abbas Magomadov."

"Yeah... Here's the thing. I understood Magomadov was dead."

"That was some very clever misdirection. With the help of the Australian Secret Intelligence Organization we were able to track him to San Francisco, where he'd set up a religious cult, the United Church of Nergal. I joined the church, made a generous contribution and was flown to Baja to meet Abbas."

"So now he's in Baja."

"It seems San Francisco was a springboard for setting up the camp in Baja. They recruit members in California and invest the proceeds in the camp in Baja."

She spread her hands. "You have your mission and your instruction, and now you have your target. So what is your problem, Harry?"

"It's not a problem, Sandy. It's an opportunity. They have a small town out there in the desert. There must be over a thousand men and women there. Most of the men seem to have some kind of military background. Some of them are definitely special ops. They are well armed and well trained. Yesterday I discovered to my cost that they have started celebrating combats to the death as part of their training. They venerate Nergal, a Sumerian god of war and death."

"OK," she sounded dubious, "but I am still not clear what you want. What you are describing is a Mexican problem within Mexican jurisdiction. Besides which, presumably, if you follow your instructions and conclude your mission, the cult will disintegrate."

"Yeah, that's true, but what struck me, when I saw the devotion he commands among his men, was that Colonel Magomadov and his organization could be a positive asset to the DEA and to the Mexican authorities—not to mention the CIA and the US Government—by bringing down Sinaloa and the other cartels, and putting in their place an organization which is much easier to..." I paused and looked at my watch, then looked at her, "to cooperate with."

Her jaw dropped slightly. I nodded elaborately at her and she glanced at the brigadier on the screen. He nodded too. She squinted at me.

"You are suggesting exactly what, Harry?"

"Major, every year the Agency pulls in several billion dollars or more from illicit cooperation with Sinaloa." I saw the expression in her eyes and her mouth sagged open. I raised a finger and pointed to the watch. She closed her mouth. "That money goes into the black budget and vanishes in Iran, Afghanistan, Syria, Colombia and several other places. What I am suggesting is that we draw down a proportion of that money into a dedicated Panamanian account and funnel it to Abbas Magomadov and the Church of Nergal, on the understanding that he undertakes to destroy Sinaloa and the other cartels."

Before she could answer I added, "Why? Why would the CIA want to do that? The answer is simple. Sinaloa has become too powerful. They have penetrated Congress, the judiciary, law enforcement, border control, and they pretty much own the Mexican government. Sinaloa does not dance to our tune anymore and they have become a law unto themselves. The Agency has been aware for some time, as I am sure you know, Sandy, that Sinaloa has become a problem. Your predecessor," I said, gesturing at her, "Bill Ortega, his murder by Sinaloa was a wake-up call for all of us, wasn't it?"

"So you are suggesting that we fund this Church of Nergal as a paramilitary force to eliminate Sinaloa?"

"And the other cartels."

"So that we, through them, exercise de facto control over the Mexican government and the flow of narcotics out of Mexico."

"The proceeds from that market would supply the budget of a small nation every year."

"I take it you would run this operation."

"I would liaise between Magomadov and the Agency. The Agency would take care of the laundry and we would have in and out accounts in Panama to process the proceeds."

"Boy you've got it all figured."

I shrugged. "That's what I get paid to do. Standard operating procedure, Sandy."

While I had been talking I had been sketching a map of Baja on a scrap of paper. I had marked the position of the camp and now I raised it for the brigadier to see and handed it to the major.

"Sinaloa are complacent at the moment. They don't even know the United Church of Nergal exists. A thousand well-equipped men, trained and coordinated by an expert team, could cause untold damage to the cartels. In a couple of months, three at the most, Sinaloa could be finished and we would have total control."

Major Sandy Silverman turned and looked at the brigadier on the laptop. He had his chin resting on the heels of his hands, his fists covering his mouth and his elbows on his desk. The major was somewhere between mad and incredulous. She spread her arms, silently shaking her head. The brigadier sat back and smiled. He said, "Thank you, Bauer, that is superb work and a superb initiative. Obviously I can't sanction an operation like the one you're proposing without discussing it with Operations first. Have you discussed this with Magomadov yet?"

"Only in very broad terms. He obviously likes the idea. It could not only be lucrative, but it gets him off the hook as far as any prosecution is concerned. I would suggest a change of identity and public acknowledgement that the body found in San Francisco was indeed him."

"Agreed. How soon do you see this going into operation?"

"As soon as possible. My own situation is precarious. Abbas knows now that I work for the Agency and was dispatched to execute him. So trust is an issue. A swift decision would consolidate trust and give a pragmatic reason for cooperation." I paused and looked fixedly at the brigadier. "I would like to take the deal to Abbas tomorrow or the day after at the latest."

He nodded. "I understand."

"Another consideration is that we are here in Mexico City and he is waiting for us to return. A decision by tonight, or tomorrow at the latest would be helpful."

"Understood. Well, stand by, keep your cell by you and the major or I will be in touch with you in the next few hours. Obviously I can't guarantee that the board will buy it, but I think it stands a damn good chance."

As he spoke he raised his thumb and his image winked off the screen. The major looked at me, frowning hard. I put my finger to my lips and showed her the watch for the third time.

"Thank you, Sandy. I'll hope to hear from you by tonight or

tomorrow morning at the latest. This deal could solve a lot of problems for a lot of people." I stood and extended my hand. She took it and stood too. "I'm pretty sure the board will approve it, Harry. I'll be in touch as soon as I know something."

"I appreciate it, Sandy. I'll see myself out."

Two minutes later I stepped out into the midday sunshine, switched off the recording device and sent the recording to Abbas. Then I stuffed my hands in my pockets and made my way at a slow stroll back toward the Sheraton. Tomorrow, or the day after, I could expect a full-scale raid on the complex. I would know the full details by tonight, tomorrow morning at the very latest. Then I would kill Abbas, the dead of Novye-Yurt would be avenged. And I...

What would I do then?

I walked slowly toward my hotel and wondered.

FOURTEEN

In the lobby I found Bohdan Bob Fedorko waiting for me. He was sitting in a chair pretending to read the paper. He dropped it when he saw me, stood and crossed the floor to meet me.

"Harry, we need to talk."

"What about?" I gestured with my head toward the bar. "Let's get a beer."

"No, better we walk. Come."

I followed him out onto the Avenue Paseo de la Reforma. We crossed through the gardens to the main drag and turned left, walking in the mottled shade of the trees. He didn't say anything so I asked him, "What's on your mind?"

He took a big, deep breath and shoved his hands in his pockets.

"You have to tell me who you are, and why you are here; what you are doing."

"This again? Come on! What more can I tell you?"

"OK!" He kept walking, but turned to face me, holding up his left hand like he was telling me to stop. He had tears in his eyes.

"OK, Harry, I am going to come clean with you. Maybe it

costs me my life. Maybe I die now. But that is OK. I don't mind. Your watch is recording still?"

I took it off and handed it to him. As he inspected it I asked him, "What the hell are you talking about, Bob?"

He shoved the watch in his pocket and blurted, "I am here to kill Abbas."

I looked away at the passing traffic. "I'd kind of figured that," I told him. "Did you kill the guy at his house? His double?"

"No, he did that himself."

"How do you know?"

"He told us. Anna and me. Anna went with him, to help remove his hand. He is monster. He massacred—"

"I know about the massacres. What do you mean, you're here to kill him? How long have you been a member of the church?"

"For three months. I came from Ukraine. We received intelligence from MI6 that Abbas Magomadov had been tracked to San Francisco. So we prepared a backstory and I came to join the Church of Nergal, first to confirm it is him, and then to kill him."

I arched an eyebrow at him. "Three months? What were you waiting for, an auspicious conjunction of planets?"

"He is never alone! It is impossible to get an opportunity! That is why I need to know, are you here to kill him?"

"You need to get out of here. You need to go back to Ukraine. This is a problem I do not need right now."

"I can help you! If you are going to kill him I can help you. This man, this regiment, the Kadyrovitsy, have butchered our people, you don't know what they have done, rape children, castrate men—"

"I know what they have done—"

"They are not human! *They are monsters!*"

He was getting agitated and his voice was rising. I told him, "Shut up, Bob."

His jaw kept working, but he bit back the words he wanted to say, took a deep breath and shoved his hands back in his pockets.

I asked him, "Are you an American citizen?"

"Yes."

"Go, get on a plane, return to the States—"

"Impossible. I cannot. I was sent here to execute Abbas. I must do that or die trying. Now tell me, for God's sake, why are you here? Who are you? The truth!"

"It's none of your goddamn business, Bob. And if you keep going like this you are going to get us both killed."

He stopped, stepped toward me and grabbed my lapels in his fists.

"Is it true you are CIA? Is it true you are going to use him against Sinaloa? Is it true? This means you will protect him and pardon him his crimes!"

I spoke very quietly, taking hold of his upper arms, and looking into his eyes and smiling like we were having an intense, meaningful conversation.

"Let go of me, Bob, or I swear I will break your neck right here where you stand."

I continued to smile and after a moment he let go my lapels. "I am sorry."

"Now, we keep walking and you listen to me very carefully. You are drawing attention to us with every word you say, and every gesture you make. If Abbas has men watching us right now, we are both dead. Second, do you seriously think that, seeing your behavior right now, I would share any sensitive intel with you? You're out of control, you're a danger and a liability."

He stopped walking and turned to face me, searching my face. I turned too and, placing my hand on his shoulder, started walking slowly back toward the hotel. He was staring at his feet as he walked and suddenly gave a small laugh.

"So, I am right. You are here going to kill him."

"No, Bob, and you better get a grip before we get back to the hotel. Understand this—I am tired of killing. You understand that? And by the time we get back to the Nergal camp, I am going to be Abbas's right-hand man in charge of security. You know that and I know that. And if you keep mouthing off the way you are and acting crazy, I am going to have to kill you. Do you understand that? Do you understand that?"

He didn't answer. He just walked and watched me. I figured I'd take that as a yes.

"So you have three options." I held up three fingers to prove it. "Get the hell out of here and go back to the US, or stay but keep your moth shut and stay out of my way."

We walked a few paces and he glanced at me. "Or...?"

"Die."

We got back to the hotel. Bob was subdued and went to his room. As I was opening the balcony there was a knock on the door. Before I could say anything it opened and Primitivo the pigrilla stood looking at me. I crossed the room and stood a couple of inches from him, looking him in the eye. He had the kind of primal intelligence in his eyes you find sometimes in rocks.

"I thought I explained to you, Primitivo, about knocking at doors."

He wasn't real interested. He studied my face a moment and grunted, "Master tell me to keep eyes on you. I keep eyes on you."

"You keep eyes on me, Primitivo, but when you knock at my door you wait till I invite you in. Do you understand?"

There was no reaction. He held my eye, but after a moment he said, "Master want you alive. When time come for you to die, I am gonna break your back, and while you are dying, I am gonna cut you open and strangle you with your own intestines. You got a big mouth, but you are a little man. You go out, you tell me."

He stepped out and closed the door. His reaction had surprised me for a couple of reasons. Not least because he seemed to assume Abbas was going to have me killed before long. I also figured that if Abbas confided in anybody, it would be in the stupidest, least threatening people around him. Least threatening for him. Because I figured Primitivo the pigrilla was probably a lot more dangerous than he looked. And he looked pretty dangerous.

The rest of the day passed without incident, and I spent most of it lying on my bed staring at the blue, Mexican sky and thinking about Abbas Magomadov and the pigrilla. Occasionally, when I closed my eyes to concentrate, I thought about Sam— Salambek Bazurkaev—who had called me and then vanished; and when I thought of him I was drawn back to the house on Manzanilla Avenue, and that unsettling feeling that I had missed something, something important.

At some point I drifted off to sleep, and when I opened my eyes again the light outside had turned copper. In my mind I could hear the cicadas, the laughter on the evening air and the imagined tinkling of ice in tall glasses. I sat up, half in a trance. The sign by the gate said, "Eden," the gate was open—pulled to, but open. So I had gone in. The house had been still and empty. Dusk was falling and I could hear the pool lapping in back. The sliding, plate-glass doors had been pulled to, like the gate, but left open.

Left open to allow access, or because somebody had left in a hurry. In my mind I went inside. The room had been dark. Not black, but dusk-dark, where the shadows fused into each other. Upstairs was the body, made to look like Abbas's body. But it was not his. It belonged to somebody who was not on any of the Five Eyes databases.

But I didn't know any of that yet. I was still downstairs in those open-plan rooms, what modern architects called spaces. There was a big dining-room-cum-sitting-room which extended into a kitchen with a breakfast bar and stools. Everything was clean and tidy, well ordered, but there were no family pictures and no photo albums, no sign of children or a woman.

I froze. No sign of a woman. My pulse had accelerated. But there was. There was a trace of a woman. And as it dawned on me I replayed in my mind the conversation I had had with Sam, Salambek Bazurkaev, and in that moment my cell began to ring. I snatched it up and saw it was the embassy.

"Yeah."

It was Major Sandy Silverman. "Mr. Bauer, this is Sandy, can you speak?"

"Yes."

"You have the go-ahead."

"I need a date and a time so I can coordinate."

"I'm about to patch you through to your brigadier."

"Harry."

"Most people do that, right?"

"What are you talking about, Harry?"

"The major did it, now you just did it—"

"Did what? You said my name, confirmed it was me."

"Of course I did, what the devil are you on about?"

"Never mind. When does it go down?"

"The day after tomorrow at midday. You have a little less than forty-eight hours. More like forty-five. Are you all right?"

"Yeah, did you or that outfit from the Pentagon—"

"ODIN, they are not from the Pentagon."

"Yeah, those guys. Did they ever trace Salambek Bazurkaev?"

"No. Is it important?"

"What about the cuts, when he hacked the body? A sword, right?"

"Yes, probably a very sharp sword. What's on your mind?"

"I can't talk right now. You going to give me a signal?"

"Yes. You'll know."

"OK, see you on the other side."

I hung up and went to look for Bob. I hammered hard on his door and the pigrilla and his pigrilla pal came out into the corridor to look at me. The door opened and Bob stood blinking at me. I pushed him inside, went in after him and closed the door. I waited five seconds and it opened again. I knew it was going to and I was ready. I wrenched it open all the way and kicked Primitivo hard in the balls with my instep. He looked real surprised. His eyes bulged and his face started to crumple. As he bent forward, clutching the only part of him that wasn't made of solid granite, I twisted my right foot, flicked my hip and drove a right hook right through his head. If he'd been a bit more flexible he might have ridden it, but he had a neck like a redwood and his head took the full impact.

His jaw sagged and his eyes lost focus. He said quietly, "Oh..."

I took his shoulder gently and guided him toward the stairs beside the elevators. His pal, Ernesto, was watching me with a confused frown on his pigrilla face. I positioned Primitivo at the top of the stairs where he stood knock-kneed and sobbing, and I kicked him hard in the ass. He thudded down one flight of steps and lay weeping at the bottom. I turned to Ernesto. "You want some?" He shook his head. I said, "Good. Go help your friend. Leave me alone. If I need you, I'll call you. Pack your bags, we go in an hour or two at the most."

Bob was at the door, watching me. He looked like a man watching a movie in a dead language. I pushed him inside again and closed the door.

"We have the go-ahead. A couple of officers from the CIA will come to Nergal the day after tomorrow to conclude the deal with Abbas."

He sat on the bed. He looked disappointed. "It's true then."

"Of course it's true. Central Intelligence couldn't have imagined a situation like this in their wildest wet dreams. It's tailor made for them."

"What about Abbas? Do you trust him?"

I rolled my eyes. "Stop trying to entrap me, Bob. I have made my position on Abbas clear. My job was to kill him, for Christ's sake. This is business, stop wanting me to fall on my damned knees to him, like you and Anna. Now pack your bags, we're going. Call the pilot, we depart in an hour, to maximum. Got it?"

He nodded. He looked depressed. He got to his feet and moved toward his wardrobe. I paused at the door and snapped my fingers. "Who's got the watch? Did Primitivo give it to you?"

"No, he hung on to it. Why?"

I approached him, grabbed his shoulders and put my face close to his. "At the airport you get lost. Primitivo is in no condition to go after you, and Ernesto will have to stay with me. You go and you get the next flight to the States. Book it now if you can, but you go. You understand?"

He didn't react. He just looked depressed the way only Eastern Europeans know how. I heard a commotion outside and pointed at him. "Do it!"

I stepped out into the corridor and saw Ernesto helping Primitivo into his room. Primitivo was still sobbing. I pointed at them and snapped, "You have less than an hour. If you are not ready, you get left behind. Move!"

They were ready. An hour later Bob settled the bill and we got a cab to the airport. It was an hour's drive over the mountains, back to Toluca. By the time we arrived, night had fallen and the small, floodlit airfield looked strangely desolate and empty. The cab pulled up and I climbed out, followed by Bob, while Ernesto helped the still hobbling, and now badly bruised Primitivo. Bob paused a moment and watched them move toward the door.

"Why'd you do that to him?"

"I had several reasons I can't share with you, Bob, but the main one? He was getting on my nerves."

He narrowed his eyes at me. "You are one mean son of a bitch, aren't you?"

I stared at him for a moment before answering. Then I said, "Bob, you really don't want to be on this plane when it lands."

He didn't say anything. He just turned and pushed through the doors.

FIFTEEN

Bob was on the plane when we landed. He followed me down the steps into the desert night. Behind us came Ernesto and Primitivo, moving slowly and with care. There was the cool, fresh smell of salt on the air, and the soft hiss of the surf. Ahead of us, by the tower, there were a couple of Wranglers waiting. I headed for one of them, with Bob at my shoulder. He spoke quietly as we walked.

"Are you going to betray me and hand me over?"

"No, but if you do anything stupid I'll kill you." I yanked open the door of the Jeep and climbed in. As he climbed in after me I told him, "Napoleon once said, 'When in doubt, do nothing.'"

The driver looked back at me. He was in military fatigues and had a sand-colored hat on his head.

"The Master wants you to go and see him as soon as you arrive."

I nodded. "OK, good, let's go."

We pulled away as Bob slammed the door and I turned back to him.

"Of course the Duke of Wellington kicked his ass all the way from Portugal and Cadiz to Waterloo, but still it was good advice.

When in doubt...," I paused, staring him in the eye, "...*do nothing*. You understand that?"

He looked away, at the dark desert moving past. "Yeah, I understand."

We got to the big house, swung down from the Jeep and made our way up the steps to the porch. The door was open and warm light flooded out. The huge space inside was empty but for a soldier in desert fatigues holding an assault rifle across his chest. He stepped forward as we entered and jerked his chin at me.

"You, go to the Master's rooms." His glance at Bob was more contemptuous. "Not you. He will call you when he needs you."

I sensed Bob hesitate behind me. Then I heard his footsteps retreat out into the night. I brushed past the guard and climbed the stairs. I followed the corridor past my room and down the second flight, till I came to Abbas's rooms. There I knocked and didn't wait for a reply. I pushed through and closed the door behind me.

He was standing with his back to me, looking out of his open window and the distant, translucent glow of the ocean. I ignored him and made for the tray of drinks, poured myself a whiskey and sipped it.

His voice reached me, but he didn't turn to face me.

"I heard what you did to Primitivo."

"He's lucky I didn't kill him. And while we're on the subject, I am going to have to teach some manners to the guard you have downstairs." I took another slug of the whiskey and asked, "What's so urgent you couldn't wait till I'd slept and had breakfast?"

He put his hands behind his back. The gesture reminded me of Napoleon. He walked to the nest of chairs, apparently watching his feet, like he hadn't known till that moment what they did when he walked.

"I thought you had learnt on your first day here, that it doesn't have to be urgent for me to summon you in the small hours. I say you come, you come."

"You're forgetting something, Abbas."

He raised his head and arched an eyebrow at me. "I doubt that."

"These bozos all think you are the Master and some kind of god. I know you're not. I know you're a two-bit fugitive wanted for war crimes and crimes against humanity. You're not a god, Abbas, you're the worst kind of man, the kind of human garbage we are evolving away from."

There was something like a smile on his lips, but his eyes said he really wanted to kill me. "Are you in a hurry to die, Harry?"

I took another pull on the whiskey. As I set the empty glass down I shook my head. "I am just telling you not to pull that god shit with me. I know who you are and I know what you are."

"Can you say the same of yourself?" He smiled at the expression on my face. "Pour me a drink, Harry. Have another yourself."

He sat in the large leather armchair. I thought about telling him to go to hell and get his own damned drink, but decided against it. I poured him his whiskey and poured myself another. As I handed it to him he nodded his thanks.

"You are a harsh judge, Harry. But I wonder, who elected or nominated you judge? Where is your divine authority to judge that I am the lowest scum and you are so far superior that you can execute me? Who gives you this entitlement?"

"Me."

He laughed out loud. "Then maybe you are the god here!"

I felt a sudden, irrational irritation with all the stupidity I had around me. It was like walking into your study, or your living room and finding everything is a mess and nothing is where it should be.

"God? What is this obsession you people have with gods? You're a person! You eat, you drink, you shit and you piss just like all those morons out there. In fact, the only power you have is the power they give you through their own damned stupidity."

He nodded. "The man they imagine I am is a god. They have projected their need for a god onto me. What makes me different

THE UNAVENGED | 129

from them, Harry, is that I accept it, and by some kind of divine alchemy, I become a god."

"Bullshit."

"Men like you killed the gods."

"Good."

I was about to drain my glass and leave, but he said, "Do you know what a dimension is, Harry?"

I sighed. "I am tired and I would like to go to bed."

"Bear with me. What is a dimension?"

"You're going to tell me now that you come from another dimension? Up and down, across, depth…"

"Anything you can measure is a dimension."

"OK, congratulations, was there anything else?"

"Einstein said that time was the fourth dimension of space, but he was wrong."

I screwed up my face at him. "What the hell are you talking about, Abbas?"

"Time," he said simply. "Einstein realized that time was another way of measuring space. You measure movement through space, that's time."

"So what?"

"He was wrong."

I sat opposite him. "Einstein was wrong, and you know this because you are a god?"

"Time is the fifth dimension of space. Gravity is the fourth." He leaned back and sighed, like my stupidity was boring him. He spread his hands. "When you create space, you automatically create the potential to contract and expand. And so everything begins to contract toward the center. That's gravity. We measure it as weight. That's the fourth dimension."

He sat forward and smiled, shaking his head. "People think dimensions are parallel universes. They are not. Dimensions are ways of measuring our world. But here's the thing, Harry. The higher the dimension, fifth, sixth, seventh, the more those measurements become subjective."

"You're not losing me, Abbas. I never started following you. What the hell are you talking about?"

"First we measure space in simple distance, inches, feet, yards, miles. Then we measure it in weight, gravity, then time, what comes next?"

"I don't know."

"Pain." He clenched his fist and opened it. "Contraction and expansion, tension, pain. And so it continues, through higher and higher dimensions of suffering and pleasure until finally we escape the three-dimensional world completely and move into the two-dimensional world of the mind. Pure mind."

I stared at him a while nodding, then drained my glass. "The mind you are completely out of." I stood. "Tomorrow, the day after at the latest, a couple of Company men—CIA officers—will come for a meeting with you to nail down the details of the agreement."

"I heard the recording."

"You're welcome."

I moved to the door but his voice stopped me.

"I have arrested Anna."

"Why?"

"Because I think you like her."

"I don't like her or dislike her. I think she's as crazy as you are. You think you can control me by threatening her?" His nod was barely perceptible. I said, "You're wrong. I couldn't be less interested in that woman."

"Perhaps. I don't believe you. I think you are a liar and your ultimate objective is still to kill me."

I shrugged. "Think what you like. I'll see you in the morning." I turned and opened the door, then paused and looked back at him where he sat watching me from his chair. "You want some advice?"

"No."

"Tough shit, you're going to get some anyway. You said it was better to rule in hell than to serve in heaven."

"That's true."

"But the whole point about hell is that you can't rule it. Look at you." I pointed at him. "The hell you live in is a prison of paranoia and self-delusion, lies and fantasy. How can you rule anything if you can't tell the truth from fantasy? All you know is that you're permanently terrified. So you made yourself the most exclusive category of all and pretended you were a god. But really, Abbas, you're just a frightened, confused mortal, like the rest of us."

I left and made my way to my room, feeling like a man who has just signed his own death warrant. But I was finding it hard to give a damn and I was half hoping he'd send half a dozen of his pigrillas to get me.

I let myself into my room and went to stand on the balcony, staring out at the dark, silent houses, the dirt streets and the dark form of the temple. I wondered if there was a jail, or if Anna was confined to one of the rooms. I hadn't lied to Abbas. I didn't like the woman. I thought she was crazy and there was a kind of ugliness to her, despite her beauty. But even so, I found myself worrying. Whatever she had done, I didn't want her to get hurt, and I was aware that my feelings were hypocritical.

In the end I had a long shower and went to bed.

The hammering on my door came just before the dawn. I swung out of bed, pulled on my jeans and wrenched open the door. It was the same guard who'd told me to go and see Abbas alone.

"You again."

"The Master want you at the temple. Ten minutes."

I closed the door in his face and went to have a cold shower. When I was fully awake I threw the Chinese kung fu suit on the bathroom floor and pulled on my jeans and my boots. I did up my shirt as I went down the stairs. The guard was by the door looking like his life wasn't what he'd asked for for Christmas.

"Go!" he snapped when he saw me. "Go now!"

I figured three times was enough, so I walked over and looked down at the middle of his chest. That disconcerted him. "Listen, pal, why don't you take a holiday from yourself. It'll do you good."

I locked eyes with him and his voice became shrill. "Go! You go!"

Suddenly I got mad. I gripped the barrel of the rifle with my right hand, gripped his throat with my left and began to squeeze. His eyes bulged, more with alarm than lack of oxygen. I put my face up close to his and snarled, "Next time you shout at me, you had better be ready to use this rifle, because if you don't shoot me, I am going to rip off your head and spit down your throat."

I thought that would satisfy me, but it didn't. So I smashed a right hook through his head and left him lying making odd, glottal noises on the floor.

By the time I got to the temple it was full. Everyone turned and watched me enter. I ignored them and stood looking at the throne. It was empty, but there was a chair to the left, on the floor beside it. Over on my left, to the right of the throne, I saw Bob. He was on his knees, with his head hanging forward.

I was about to go over to him and ask him what was going on, but I heard movement behind me and turned. Abbas was approaching with his nine guards. He ignored me and made his way to the throne, where he settled himself, surrounded by his soldiers. He looked down at Bob.

"Mr. Prosecutor, are you ready for the accused?"

"Yes, Master."

The guard on Abbas's right-hand side took a step forward and bellowed, "*Bring the accused!*"

Now there was a noise out in the darkness, like un-oiled hinges creaking. A door banged and there was the sound of feet trudging through sand. I knew what to expect. I knew what I was going to see; but still my gut burned where she appeared out of the darkness into the light of the temple. She wasn't bruised and didn't appear to be hurt, but her face was swollen from crying and her eyes were raw and red. There were two guards with her and as they entered the temple the one on her right shoved her so she ran a few steps forward. In front of Abbas's throne she dropped to her knees, sobbing.

He said, "What have you to say?"

She looked up at him. It was pathetic and I felt a crazy rage inside me. She was shaking her head.

"Master, I would never betray you. You are everything to me, I would rather die than betray you. Please believe me. I love you more than my self. How can I prove it to you? I will do anything."

He looked out into the crowd. "But there is nothing you can do. Perhaps somebody else can prove it for you. Bohdan Fedorko will be your prosecutor, and if he is successful you will be executed at dawn. So we must get a move on. Now, we must find you a defense counsel. Take her to the chair."

This last was addressed to the two soldiers who dragged her, still sobbing, to her feet and to the chair beside the throne. There they dumped her and stood guard beside her.

I knew what was coming next. Abbas's eyes found me and he regarded me with smiling poison in his eyes.

"Harry, Mr. Bauer. You expressed to me last night your complete indifference toward Anna Molyboha. So, as we know that justice must be blind and impartial, perhaps you would be so kind as to defend her in these proceedings."

I shook my head. He gave a small laugh.

"Forgive me, I have not expressed myself clearly. It was not a request, but rather a requirement. Mr. Fedorko will conduct her prosecution, and you will conduct her defense. Please, approach."

I crossed the floor among the sitting faithful and stood in front of the throne.

"What is she accused of?"

"Treason, Mr. Bauer. She is accused of conspiring with others in a plot to murder the Master. If she is found guilty, she will be tortured in ways you cannot imagine, to give up the names of her co-conspirators. So you would be very wise, Harry, to put up a very spirited defense."

SIXTEEN

ABBAS SAID: "THE PROSECUTION WILL MAKE ITS CASE."

It seemed to me that Bob took a long time to get to his feet, but finally he raised his head and stood. He looked at Abbas and said, "Yes, Master." Then he turned to the assembled crowd of well over a thousand people crammed into every corner of the temple, and raised his voice.

"Anna Molyboha, the secretary of the United Church of Nergal, is accused of conspiring with one or more people to assassinate our Master. Our Master, in his endless compassion and his love of truth, has charged me with finding evidence that will prove, beyond any doubt, that this woman is guilty of the crime with which she is charged."

He paused and stared down at the rug under his feet.

"I will begin by explaining to you exactly how Anna went about executing her plan. Then I will prove each step." He raised his head and took a step toward the crowd. "You must know that for many years our Master has been hunted across continents, across the world, by the forces of international evil, because he is perceived by them as a danger to their empire of brainwashing, consumerism and exploitation. Always, since he left Chechnya and crossed into Georgia, our master has stayed several steps ahead of his pursuers, outwitting them and out-thinking them at every turn. Until, some years ago, in Australia he convinced the authorities that he had died, and from there, following the star of his destiny, he traveled to San Francisco where he established the United Church of Nergal under the very noses of the empire of international evil, the United Satanists of America.

"And here it was that he recruited the treacherous woman who would attempt to kill him. Anna Molyboha, who claimed to be from Chechnya and claimed to be his faithful devotee and his most faithful disciple."

He walked up to her and looked down into her face. She was still sobbing, shaking her head and repeating ad nauseam, "It isn't true, please don't believe him."

"In reality Anna Molyboha had been recruited by Interpol many years before to hunt for so-called war criminals, ignoring the war crimes of their own paymasters. She had followed the Master to Australia, and when his body was found, she knew that he was too clever, too resourceful and too strong to have died in the outback in such a way. And she hunted and investigated tirelessly until she found the clues she was looking for, that told her that our master had escaped to California, and she followed him there. And when she saw that he had founded a church, to give spiritual guidance to the lost and the suffering, she attempted to exploit his holy, divine work as a way to get close to him."

He moved and came and stood in front of me, not looking at me but looking out at the crowd.

"And soon, when the master had given her work as his secretary, giving her the opportunity to free herself from evil and choose the right path, instead of this she communicated with her employers and had them send at least one agent, perhaps more, to infiltrate the church and murder our master."

He glanced at me and moved away, addressing the crowd again. "You know that the master will not torture or execute a person who has not been found guilty at trial. And so it is your obligation here today to find Anna Molyboha guilty of this evil crime, so that she can be tortured by the Master's guards, and forced to tell who her co-conspirators are."

I had had enough and I raised my voice, shouting to Abbas where he sat on his throne.

"Abbas, this is bullshit and you know it. That woman is devoted to you. She has never done anything to harm you and you, and Bob and everybody here knows that to be the truth. Call off this trial and release Anna right now. This is just plain stupid!"

Bob gave a short laugh and turned to face me. "Is that your defense? Surely, Master," and he turned for the first time to face Abbas, "surely the poverty of the defense proves the case for the prosecution!"

Abbas smiled and raised a questioning eyebrow at me.

"What have you to say, Harry? Is that your defense?"

"No, it's not my damned defense. I am just appealing to you to stop this madness. She has done nothing to you! The only person here who has conspired to kill you is me. You know that!"

"Yes," he said mildly. "I know that. But you changed your mind, didn't you? Perhaps you forgot to inform Interpol."

I was going to tell him that Interpol did not organize assassinations, but realized that this trial had nothing to do with truth or conspiracies. This trial was about power, and making me see—me and the supposed CIA agents who would be coming later that day or tomorrow—that he was king and he could do whatever the hell he liked. So I turned to Bob and asked him, "All right, Bob. What's your evidence against her?"

He nodded and walked over to face Anna.

"Anna Molyboha, is it not true that when you were seventeen years of age you fled from Chechnya and sought asylum in United States?"

She nodded. "Yes, My family were killed—"

"Just answer yes or no. And is it not true that you were soon recruited by CIA to work for them and spy on Russia?"

She nodded again, glancing up at Abbas. "Yes, I have told the Master this..."

"And is it not true that when Master escaped from Chechnya and ascended to godliness," his voice began to rise, "you were seconded by CIA to Interpol to track him down and find him?"

"No!"

"See how she lies!" I knew what he was doing and I didn't like it. He turned to the crowd and pointed at her. "See! Yes, she escaped from Chechnya! Yes, she worked for CIA! But when I ask her the key question, she lies!"

She was shaking her head, crying out loud, "*No! It's not true!*"

""Do you also deny that you followed him to Australia?"

"I have never been—"

"Do you also deny that the Australian Security Intelligence Organization assisted you in tracking the Master down?"

"*Please, Master please, I have never—*"

"Do you deny that they supplied you with intelligence and equipment, and allowed you to inspect the Passport Offices records?"

"I have never, never been to Australia... Master, please, I have told you everything..."

"See!" He turned to the crowd again. "See how she lies through her teeth! See how she appeals to the Master for mercy, because she knows she is lying!"

I cut in. "You said you were going to supply proof. All I've seen is you shouting and asking questions which she has answered. Where's your proof she ever set foot in Australia, Bob?"

"You want proof?" He nodded at me and turned back to Anna. "Is it true, Anna Molyboha, that when the Master arrived in San Francisco you went to meet him and offer your services?"

"Yes."

He barked a loud, obnoxious laugh. "So can you tell us please, how you knew that he was in San Francisco?"

"I saw his photograph."

He repeated the words, slowly and deliberately, "You saw...his photograph? You *saw* his photograph. And tell us, please, *where* did you see his photograph, if not in the file you were supplied by Interpol?"

"I saw his face in local free newspaper, that he was buying church. I had seen him in Chechnya. He came to our town with Kadyrovitsy, looking for rebels, and..." She trailed off, looking up at Abbas, "and I knew then that I love him."

Bob turned to me and spread his arms wide. "You want more proof? She has been obsessed with the Master since she was a teenager, she has admitted obtaining intelligence in San Francisco and coming to the church to offer her services, so that she could be close to him and assassinate him. Anyone, honestly, anyone who cannot see that, is willfully blind!"

I stared at him, feeling the hot coals of anger burning in my gut. I spoke quietly.

"What are you doing, Bob? What is this? Is this what you've become?"

"I am not on trial, here!"

I arched an eyebrow at Abbas, but spoke to Bob. "Are you sure?"

Abbas said, "Confine your comments and questions to the case, Harry."

"May I question the witness?"

He made a question with his face and showed it to Bob. Bob said, "The prosecution rests its case, Master."

I moved to Anna, who was doubled up weeping into her hands.

"Anna, I need you to be brave. I am going to ask you some questions, and I need you to answer honestly and from the heart, OK?"

She raised her sodden face to mine and nodded.

"When was the first time you ever saw the man you know as the Master, Anna?"

"A few years ago, in Chechnya. He came to our village with the Kadyrovitsy. They killed so many people. They were going to kill me, but the Master came and he saved me. He did not allow them to kill me."

"What happened after that?"

She looked away, into her memories. "Some soldiers came and took me, and gave me to General Babanin. He is a disgusting old man and he made me have sex with him. I was a slave for him."

"Is that why you escaped?"

She nodded. "Yes."

"Did you blame the Master for what happened? Did you want to seek revenge on him?"

"No, no!" She was shaking her head. "No! He saved me. I dreamed of him every day and every night, coming back to save me again. But he could not."

"Why?"

"Because he had found the light, and he too had to escape."

"So what did you do?"

"I escaped. First Georgia, then Turkey, like the Master. But then from Turkey I went to Greece and there to American embassy. I showed them scars and told them my story, and they gave me refugee status. Destiny brought me to San Francisco, where I found the Master again and could give him my life in thanks for saving me."

I looked up at Abbas. He was watching me, but showed no sign of being moved by her story, or her obvious sincerity.

"How did you come to work for the CIA, Anna?"

"I won a scholarship to go to university in San Francisco. One professor there introduced me to a woman who was from CIA. She asked me if I want to make some extra money and also help people who are in trouble, like I was. I said yes. So they ask me to look at Chechen websites, read Chechen papers, and when my degree is finish they say they will send me to Washington. But it never happened."

"Did they ever second you to Interpol and send you to Australia?"

"Never! Never, never, never!"

I turned to Bob. "Have you one witness—*one*—who can place Anna anywhere outside of the United States after she came here as a refugee? Have you *one shred of evidence* that she was ever seconded to Interpol?" I advanced toward him, pointing at him. "I'll go further, Bob. Have you *any shred of evidence that Interpol were ever involved in the search for Colonel Abbas Magomadov?*" He stared at me. Before he could answer I turned back to Abbas. "He can't! But I can. I can prove that this woman *never* worked for Interpol and was never used by the CIA to search for you. And you know—*you know*—that I can prove it. Because I was involved in that investigation and I was the man detailed to assassinate you. I know what agency carried out the investigation and it was not the Central Intelligence Agency, and it was definitely not Interpol. So I can state categorically that this woman is *not* guilty, and if anybody here is guilty of conspiring to kill you, it is *me!*" I stared at him a moment and added, "And you *know* that!"

There was an enormous silence. You could feel its weight pressing down on the congregation, on all those people assembled in the temple. Things had not played out as Abbas had planned, or as Bob had planned either. But having dragged Anna from the jaws of death, I now had to make Death close its jaws, at least for now. So I turned to the stunned crowd and said, pointing back at Abbas:

"And you know *why* he knows? Because he has the sight, he has the light of truth in his mind and in his soul. Because when these accusations were brought against his most faithful servant, he understood that her accuser and the accusations he brought, had to be exposed in the light of public judgment. He sees!" I said, pointing at him again. "He sees into people's hearts and people's minds, and he knows what is there. And this man, this god, our master, knows that this woman has never felt anything but love, gratitude and devotion for him." I shook my head. "She is not only not guilty of the crimes she is accused of. She is innocent, and a heroine in her own right."

I turned to face Abbas, who was regarding me through

hooded eyes. "Master," I said, "you have demonstrated yet again your wisdom and the clarity of your mind. I beg of you now to release this woman, your most faithful and devoted servant, from these charges. As well as your wisdom and your justice, your humanity, your kindness and your compassion are renowned among your people. Bless this woman now, take her to your bosom, forgive her her trespasses and set her free."

He arched his eyebrow and nodded slowly. "You should have been a lawyer, Harry, or an orator. A moving speech, clever, and a clever use of an absolute absence of evidence. It is true, you told me you had been sent by the CIA to assassinate me. I know from my men, and from the recording you sent me, that you had a meeting at the embassy with CIA officers. So who would know better than you whether Anna was working for the CIA to investigate me? You have convinced me, and, as you say, my clarity of sight made all of this apparent to me from the start. I had but to look into my child's soul to know that she was pure." He turned to Anna. "You will not be executed today, my Anna. Tonight you will sleep with me and show me your gratitude."

She sagged and fell to the floor at his feet, sobbing and crying out her thanks. I looked over at Bob. I wondered if he knew what was coming. Abbas ignored Anna and turned to Bob.

"You, on the other hand, my Ukrainian friend, bring only darkness and lies to me. You have betrayed me, with jealousy in your heart and lies in your mouth. You have tried today to kill my most faithful servant. If her life is spared today, yours will pay for hers. You will be executed at dawn."

Bob went pale. He shook his head. Abbas turned to the two guards standing beside Anna and pointed at Bob. "Take him to the cell!"

Then he pointed at me. "And you, Harry, you will be his executioner!"

SEVENTEEN

HE TRIED TO RUN, BUT THE CROWD SURGED TO GRAB him and in seconds the guards were on him. I saw the punching, slapping and kicking start and bellowed at them. "Stop! *Stop that!*" They ignored me and I turned to Abbas and snarled. "You want me to execute him, make them stop!"

He stood and his voice rang out, "Stop!"

The crowd backed up and the guards dragged Bob away. He was bleeding from his nose and one eye was swollen and turning purple. I was thinking on my feet and thinking fast. I advanced on the crowd, bellowing at them, "*Who is named as the executioner? You?*" I pointed at one guy, then pointed at another, "*You?*" I pounded my chest with my fist and roared, "*I was! So back off!*"

Then I turned toward the throne, where Abbas was still standing, looking down on a scene which was slowly slipping from his control. I offered him back that control, praying silently he would take the bait.

"Master, I know from personal experience that this man has not been a coward. He has been brave, and if he has failed you it has been by loving you too well. I ask compassion of you, and that you allow him to die as a warrior, fighting for his life. I will kill him with my own hands, but let him die fighting."

Abbas held my gaze in his. He knew that if he agreed, he took back control. If he refused I would become an even bigger pain in his ass. He took the easy way out.

"You do not need to tell me this, Harry. That was my judgment already." He addressed the crowd. "Until now, Bohdan has been a loyal and faithful servant, but jealousy has twisted him against my beloved Anna and corrupted his soul. For that he must die, but as befits a courageous warrior, he will die fighting so that he may redeem himself before Nergal." He looked down at the guards. "Take him, treat him with respect, let him be prepared for the fight by the girls."

He was dragged away, staring at me over his shoulder with wild eyes. The crowd began to disperse and Abbas descended from the small dais. He ignored Anna who was staring at him with a broken, weeping face, but said to me, "Follow me."

I walked next to him, with his nine guards surrounding us, as we walked back toward the house. He spoke quietly.

"That was not what I intended, Harry."

"I know."

"This deal you have arranged with the CIA had better work out. I am growing tired of you. I do not trust you, and I am not sure I like you very much anymore."

"Stop, please. You're going to break my heart."

He glanced at me and gave my face the once-over. "Your sense of humor doesn't help. Cross me one more time and CIA deal or no, I will kill you, with my own hands."

I gave him a smile that was as bland as it was insolent. "That's something to look forward to, then. Was there anything else?"

"Yes."

We had arrived at the big house and he ascended the wooden steps. On the porch he stopped and turned to me. "Go and prepare for the execution. We will meet at the field in half an hour. I will not be satisfied with Bohdan's simple death. I want you to make an example of him. This will be a show, a spectacle, a lesson and a warning."

"All those things? At once?"

Something shifted in his eyes and they became hard, more than ruthless, they became pitiless.

"I am warning you, Harry. Stop before it's too late."

I nodded. "I hear you, Master. I'll go and get ready."

I watched him and his guards climb the stairs. I poured myself a whiskey while I gave them time to get to his quarters, then I went up to look for Bob's room. I found it at the end of a dogleg to the left of my room. I paused outside his door, listening. All I could hear was silence, so I opened the door and went in. He was lying facedown on a massage couch and there were three Japanese girls giving him a massage. I wondered if Chechen heaven was more particular than regular Islamic heaven, and you got seventy-two Japanese virgins.

The girls turned to look at me. I said, "Beat it, give us ten minutes."

They made little bowing-bobbing motions and I wondered how nice girls like that wound up in places like this. I searched my memory and came up with, "*Atchi itte kudasai.*"

They giggled, I bowed, they bowed and filed out giggling and I said, "*Domo arigatogozaimasu.*"

That made them giggle even more. I closed the door and turned to Bob. He had sat up on the couch and was watching me with a face that was sour, defeated and self-pitying.

"Have you come to kill me?"

I put my foot on a chair against the wall and removed the Fairbairn and Sykes fighting knife from my boot, sheath and all.

"I have been told to make an example of you. He wants your death to be a show, a spectacle, a lesson and a warning. What the hell were you trying to do out there?"

He shook his head. "I realized you were not going to execute him or punish him for his crimes, and neither could I get close enough to kill him. He is always surrounded by guards, and in any case he is a highly skilled fighter himself. But I had to do some-thing, so I thought, he depends on Anna for practically everything. He does not acknowledge it, but she is his rock. She organizes everything, advises him, manages his time, everything. So I thought if I created discord between them..."

"So you told him that she was organizing a plot against him."

"He is so paranoid he would believe anything. I told him..." He glanced at me and hesitated.

"You told him it was no coincidence that she had introduced me to the Church, and that she had contacted the CIA to tell them where he was."

"Yes."

"Fantastic."

He jerked his head at the knife. "What are you going to do with that?"

"I ought to stick it in your fucking heart for being such a goddamn asshole." His frown was more one of confusion and incomprehension than annoyance. I threw him the knife and he caught it. He stared at it a moment. Then stared at me. I gave him a sour smile. "Put it on your ankle under your Chinese pants. And no, it's not so you can kill me with it." I pointed at his window. "It'll be dawn soon. You better get dressed."

The Japanese girls were waiting patiently outside. We did some more bowing and bobbing and giggling and I told them with gestures that Bohdan Fedorko was all done and finished and they should go away.

"*Doko ka ni itte!*" I told them, shooing them away with my hands. "*Iku! Iku!*"

I once, briefly had a Japanese girlfriend and she often told me to go away, so I learnt various ways of saying it. They hurried away in a delightful little panic and I returned to my room.

In my room I went to the balcony and stared out into the predawn darkness. I visualized the field with its posts supporting the ropes. Abbas would be at the end, on his throne, and Anna would be seated beside him. His nine guards would be deployed, three at either side and three guarding his back.

I stripped off my jeans and my shirt and my boots. The

Chinese Kung Fu suit was still on the floor in the bathroom. I put it on and slipped my Sig Sauer into my waistband behind my back. With the voluminous, baggy jacket it was invisible. Finally I stuffed a handkerchief from my jacket into my pocket.

Barefoot I made my way downstairs and along the wide dirt street to the temple and the field beside it. It was still dark and there was nobody there yet. I found the stake I had ripped loose when I had killed Olaf. It had been set back in the ground, but the earth around it was loose. I pulled the Sig from my waistband, wrapped it in the handkerchief and dug a small hole in the dirt beside the loose post. I slipped the Sig in the hole, covered it in sand, and taking off my jacket I dumped it on top. Then I went to the center of the tatami and sat cross-legged, meditating and waiting for the bloodthirsty crowd to arrive.

They began to show up after about half an hour, as the sky started turning gray in the east. They took up their places around the tatami. Those closest sat, the latecomers stood. And as the sun emerged and spilled red blood over the horizon, Abbas arrived in his white robe, surrounded by his praetorian guard. They positioned themselves as always, and he ascended to the throne. There he sat and said, "Bring the condemned man."

They must have been waiting just down the road, because thirty seconds later Bohdan Fedorko arrived. His hands were bound behind his back. Two guards accompanied him, shoved him into the tatami under the ropes and came in after him to cut his bonds. Holding his arms they turned him around to face Abbas.

"Bohdan, my old friend, how this saddens me. You have betrayed me, your Master, and now you must pay the price. You will die here today, as a lesson to all those who would betray me. Understand that treason never prospers. And the price for treason is death."

If he was quoting Shakespeare, I knew from the brigadier that he'd got it wrong, but I wasn't about to tell him. Instead I took a couple of steps toward him and asked, "What happens if he wins?"

Abbas smiled, then laughed. "I have seen you fight, Harry, and I know your spirit. You and I know, and Bohdan knows, he will not win. You will kill him. That is my decision." He shifted his attention to Bohdan. "Have you made your peace, Bohdan? Are you ready for the great transformation?"

Bohdan nodded. "Yes, Master, I am ready."

"So, begin."

The gong sounded and he moved in on me. He'd seen action and in a street brawl he'd probably have made out OK. Like a lot a fighters he hunched, looking for an opportunity to go for a takedown. I paused, giving him the opportunity. He rushed and as he rushed I stepped forward and drove a straight right into his face. It wasn't enough to take him down. It probably didn't even hurt much, but it looked good and it made his nose bleed. He staggered back, blinking, then approached again, more cautiously. But I could see from his face that he wasn't thinking about my weaknesses. Instead he was looking for the opportunity to use the three or four tricks he'd learned.

I shuffled forward quick, flicked a front kick at his shin and as my foot touched the tatami I jabbed him in the face again with my right and instantly drove my left into his chest. As he staggered back I smacked the side of his head with the back of my right fist and then drove two very showy hooks, left and right into his floating ribs. None of the blows hurt much, but they were fast and they gave the crowd something to cheer at. Ben stumbled back and fell on the mat.

I walked away and thumbed my nose, putting on a show. Ben got to his feet. I could see the rage in his eyes and I hoped he wasn't going to do anything stupid. He roared and ran at me. I let him grab me around the waist, lift me and hurl me to the mat. On the way down I put him in a headlock and we fell in a heap, with him trying to extract his head from the crook of my elbow. I rolled him over and thrust my head down beside his, like I was trying to choke him, and rasped in his ear.

"I am going to lead you back, toward the throne. Make your play, I'll back you up."

Then I let him slip out from my grip. As he staggered away from me I got to my feet. He came at me again and I backed up toward the throne. He threw a couple of punches which I weaved away from and then slapped him hard in the face. I knew I was making him mad. I was making him mad because I wanted him mad. The sun was molten bronze on the horizon, and I had no idea when the cavalry was going to show. That meant that Ben and I had one hell of a fight on our hands, armed with one Sig Sauer and a Fairbairn and Sykes fighting knife.

I needed him good and mad. So I slapped him again. He charged, raging and I stepped to my left, toward my jacket and the damaged post. He followed, charging, swinging his fists and trying to put together combinations. But he had never learned to combine his fists with his feet. As he reeled and stumbled, I trapped his right arm across his chest with my left hand and slapped him hard, twice, open-handed, then put my open hand over his face and shoved him back.

When he came at me again he was out of his mind, reaching for my face with hands like claws. I stepped outside his right arm, grabbed his wrist and kicked his feet from under him so he landed in a heap. He was twelve or fifteen feet from the throne. He glared up at me and I said, "OK, Ben, the exhibition is over. Time for the kill."

I saw the understanding dawn in his eyes, and with it the fear. I turned away and walked to my jacket. As I bent to pick it up I heard Ben's voice behind me.

"I am going to kill you, you son of a bitch!"

I paused, frowning and turned back to him. He was standing, his legs akimbo, holding the knife in his right hand. But he was not facing Abbas. He was not addressing Abbas. He was facing me, and talking to me.

I searched his eyes and decided he was serious. I took a step toward him but he was already charging. He covered the distance between us in less than a couple of seconds. He slashed at my face and I weaved back. He slashed backhanded at my neck and I backed away and moved behind him. He lunged like he was fencing and I backed away again. Then he did something unexpected. He hooked his right leg behind mine, rammed me with his shoulder and sent me sprawling to the mat. Then he was on top of me, forcing the knife down toward my throat with both hands. I held his wrists, but felt them slipping. I stared into his eyes, asking him what the hell he was doing. And the answer was clear. He was going to kill me.

EIGHTEEN

I HAD NO CHOICE BUT TO KILL HIM. IT WOULD BE A
fraction of a second. Gauge out his eyes, shift to the left, take the
knife and cut his throat. I released his left wrist to stab at his eyes,
but instead of driving down harder he sat upright, stood and
hurled the knife at the nearest of Abbas's guards. It was an expert
throw and the knife buried itself deep in the man's chest. Ben was
close behind it. The crowd watched in stunned silence as the
guard crumpled to the ground and Ben took his assault rifle and
riddled the two guards behind the first with a shower of hot lead.

He did not then turn the weapon on Abbas. Maybe he should
have. Instead he sprayed the legs of the throne and through them
the six remaining praetorian guards. By that time I was across the
field lunging for my jacket and the Sig. I heard the crowd gasp,
then scream. As I turned I saw Ben beating Abbas to the ground
with the butt of his rifle, in front of Anna. She screamed and
threw herself across him as the crowd began to surge. Ben was not
fazed. He dropped the rifle, picked up another with a full maga-
zine and fired into the crowd. The warriors of Nergal backed
away, screaming and falling over each other.

Ben turned and marched up to Abbas who turned his face
away and held up his hands, like they could ward off bullets. I

took the Sig and stood, wondering if the mighty god Abbas was remembering the hundreds of people he had shot and killed as they cowered in the very position he was in now.

Anna was screaming hysterically, trying to protect Abbas's body with her own. I moved to where three of the guards lay dead and dying and took one of their assault rifles. I put it to my shoulder and aimed it at the crowd.

"*I don't want to kill you,*" I shouted. "*I have no quarrel with you. My business is with Abbas. Now get out of here! Now!*"

They dithered, hesitant, not sure whether to be heroes or smart. I let off three shots over their heads and they opted for smart and fled, breaking into a straggling charge toward the village.

I turned back toward Ben saying, "We need to get out of here. We need to make for the plane..."

As I spoke I saw him grab Anna by the hair and drag her off Abbas. He was rasping something half-crazy in Ukrainian or Russian, and she was screaming and crying, clinging to Abbas, who was struggling to get out from underneath her. Then everything seemed to happen at once in a series of timeless, still frames. Abbas got to his knees, looking back at Ben. Ben heaved Anna away and she fell, with her hair flying, on the bloody body of one of the guards. As she flopped down, Ben turned to look at Abbas. In the long second that they stared at each other I raised my rifle and aimed it at Abbas. Abbas shifted his weight like he was about to run. Ben took aim and past Abbas I saw Anna grabbing the sidearm of the fallen guard. I remember noting it was a Glock. She pulled it from the holster as Abbas turned away and broke into a run. Ben fired and missed. I shouted, "*Ben! Anna! No!*" and Anna, now sitting with her feet splayed out in front of her, aimed the Glock with both hands and fired three, four five, six times. And as Ben fell to the ground she continued firing, as she scrambled to her feet and went after Abbas.

He was no more than fifty paces away. It was an easy shot, and with an assault rifle he would be hard to miss. But as I raised the weapon to my shoulder I saw Anna turn and take aim at me. I dropped and heard the two slugs crack overhead as they broke the sound barrier. Then she was running again, toward the disappearing form of Abbas. I took a couple of shots, but he was moving erratically and both shots went wide. I got to my feet and went after him. The thought was in my mind that he was running toward about a thousand of his loyal followers. And now so was I. That probably wasn't smart. But I also had some notion that if I seized the few minutes of chaos, I might just get him and make it to the plane before his stunned and shaken followers could get their shit together.

I ran, and I ran fast.

I made it to the big house without seeing anyone. Two got you twenty there were a thousand idiots in the garage fighting over twenty-four seats in the trucks. I wondered briefly if that was where Abbas had gone, but was pretty sure it wasn't. If I knew anything about Abbas, and I figured I knew quite a lot by then, Abbas was gathering together what pigrillas he had left to hunt me down and skin me alive.

I hoped so anyway.

If that was what he was doing, that meant he was in the big house. I ran up the steps and found the door open. I flattened against the wall and peered inside. There was nobody there. So I moved in fast and made my way to the kitchen. I found a gallon of sunflower oil and poured it liberally over every wooden surface I could find. The gas stove was fed by a large propane canister, so I opened all the taps, grabbed a couple of tea towels and a box of matches, and went to the big living room-dining room, pouring oil as I went. I dowsed the tea towels with whiskey and brandy and stuffed them into the decanters to make very expensive Molotov cocktails. Then I lit them and hurled them toward the kitchen. There were a couple of spectacular *whooshes* as the spirits ignited in blue and purple flames. Then the propane ignited and there was a bigger, hotter explosion. Then the oil caught on the wood and within seconds the ground floor was a roaring inferno. I backed toward the door, shielding my face, but a wall of flame six foot high roared across my path.

I swore violently. There was no way out unless I jumped from one of the upstairs windows. I sprinted up the wooden steps to the landing outside my bedroom. I kicked the door in and a wave of heat rushed up the stairs behind me. I was about to run for the balcony when a movement on my right made me stop and look.

Abbas and Anna had emerged from his back staircase carrying a couple of briefcases and a couple of attaché cases. They looked startled to see me. But just ahead of them were Ernesto and primitive, the original pigrilla. They didn't look startled, they looked pleased.

Pigrilla roared like a bull with an angry hornet in its pants and hurtled down the corridor toward me. I swore some more and ran into the bedroom. Through the open door I could see the flames crawling up the walls of the stairwell. As I made for the balcony to open the door Primitivo burst in with Ernesto just behind him. I raised the rifle to shoot him, but he was faster than you'd expect. He snatched the barrel and wrenched the weapon from my hands. I drove two fierce hooks into his floating ribs, right and left. I don't think he noticed. He backhanded me and sent me sprawling across the floor. My head was spinning and my ears were ringing, and I was in a lot of pain. Ernesto laughed over Primitivo's shoulder, and then in the surreal glow of the flames I saw Abbas behind Ernesto, scowling, shouting, "*Kill him! Kill him fast! We need to go!*"

Primitivo advanced toward me. Abbas and Anna squeezed past Ernesto and as Primitivo reached down and grabbed me by the scruff of the neck, Abbas heaved open the sliding glass door, forming a funnel from the open front door up to the balcony. There was a furious roar and suddenly, over Primitivo's vast shoulder I saw Ernesto screaming and bouncing as he was enveloped in flames. I felt the fierce heat wash over me and shielded my face with my arms.

I had Primitivo's huge form to protect me, but with Ernesto

writing and screaming on the floor, Primitivo had nobody to protect him. He stood suddenly erect, arching away from the door and stamping like some freakish, giant chicken. From where I was lying on the floor, with my shoulders against the wall, I slammed both my heels up into his balls, got to my feet and kicked him hard in the belly. It was like kicking ten tons of reinforced concrete. He staggered back a couple of steps and went suddenly, *whoof!* Flames enveloped him. He took another step back and fell backward over the black, motionless form of Ernesto within the flames.

The bed was smoking furiously and beginning to catch light. I knew if I stayed any longer I would catch light too, or pass out with the smoke. Abbas and Anna had disappeared and I figured they had jumped from the balcony. I went after them.

Outside there was pandemonium in the streets. The flames had spread to the roof of the building next door and it was pretty clear nobody had got around to setting up a fire service. Most people just seemed to be running, but beneath me I could see Abbas, Anna and the pilot in a jeep, with one guard holding everybody at bay with a rifle. He fired a couple of shots and the Jeep roared away toward the airstrip.

I jumped. I rolled as I landed and was too numb and dazed to notice the pain. I scrambled to my feet and ran for the back of the building. The flames had spread to the garage and a small group of guys in fatigues were scattering, screaming that the fuel barrels were going to blow. I told myself if my time had come I might as well go in a gas explosion as any other way so I ran into the inferno, screaming as I went. I could feel the heat eating at my clothes and smell the scorching of the cloth. I vaulted into the nearest Wrangler, pressed the starter and rammed it in reverse, scorching my palm as I did so. The tires screamed and I hurtled out of the flames as the place started to collapse. I braked, spun the wheel and roared down the track toward the airfield.

I hurtled across the desert with sun low on the horizon, glinting bronze off the Jeep ahead of me. A great cloud of dust rose up from the road, trailing like a plume of smoke across the sand toward the sea. I floored the pedal, not giving a damn anymore whether I crashed and burned there. I was damn sure Abbas was not getting on that plane as long as I had breath in my lungs and blood in my veins. They skidded to a halt outside the tower, kicking up gravel and stones, about two hundred yards ahead of me.

I spun the wheel savagely, skidding off the track and bouncing wildly across the dirt, heading straight for the jet. They saw too late what I intended and Abbas opened fire, strafing the Jeep. But it was too late. I was at the jet and he dared not risk damaging the plane.

I didn't stop. I didn't even slow down. I rammed the wheels under the wing doing sixty miles an hour. The whole mechanism buckled and the jet creaked and leaned over. I didn't wait. I rolled out of the Jeep, pulled the Sig from my waistband and put a bullet through the pilot's head. Abbas and Anna stopped dead fifty yards from me. Abbas raised his rifle. I didn't pause. I shot his prosthetic and the weapon jumped in the air and fell in the dirt.

He raised his hands. "All right, Harry. All right, you have proved yourself. You're quite a man. A very dangerous adversary. But think, I have done nothing to you. It is you who have turned on me. I embraced your plan. We were allies. It is still a good plan. Think! Think of what you and I can do together. We could take down Sinaloa, the Gulf, all of them! And have the support of the CIA as well. Billionaires!" He laughed. "We could truly be kings among men, gods! Think about what you are doing. You have all the cards right now. What are you going to do next?"

In the distance I could hear the soft thud of the choppers. I wondered if he had heard them. I said, "What's in the cases?"

Anna said, "Don't tell him!"

I listened to the sound of the rotors, estimated their distance. "You have about two minutes. The moment those choppers arrive, you are dead meat if you haven't told me what's in those cases."

He wasted fifteen seconds thinking about it. Then said, "Details of my offshore accounts, and five hundred thousand dollars in cash."

Anna was screaming at him to shut up. I squeezed the trigger. The Sig kicked, the back of his head exploded in a plume of pink and black gore, and after a small whiplash he sank to the desert sand.

She stood staring down at him. She had become utterly expressionless again. I said:

"You cut off his hand, didn't you?" She snapped around and stared at me, like she was surprised to find I was there. "You killed Salambek Bazurkaev, cut off his hand, and cut off Abbas's hand too. What is it, you're skilled with blades?"

She didn't answer. I went on, "It was your perfume. You were at the house the day I found his body. It was playing on my mind, when I met you at the church, it was the same perfume, jasmine and orange blossom. You didn't escape separately, did you? You planned it together, every detail. I'll even bet you were the mastermind. He chose you to be his slave, and you chose him to be your god."

Her face slowly morphed into an expression of contempt. "You know nothing. You will always know nothing. Pig shit."

The sound of the choppers was getting loud. I walked toward her, holding out my hand. "Give me the cases. Get on the ground and put your hands behind your head. Do it now."

What she did was to smash the attaché case into my face. The pain was excruciating and I reeled back. The case dropped to the sand and shards of pain shot through my brain, blinding me. By the time I had cleared my head she was clambering back into the Jeep, carrying one of the cases. She spun on a dime, kicking up huge clouds of dirt and hurtled away, north and east, just as a swarm of military helicopters burst over the horizon, accompanied by the stuttering sound of automatic gunfire.

I watched them circle over the village, around the thick columns of black smoke, and after several protracted rattling bursts I watched them start to descend. I collected up the three cases and slung them in the back of my own, damaged Jeep, as one chopper peeled off from the rest and approached the airfield. I raised a hand and waved and the helicopter came gently to rest on the tarmac, blasting me with warm air and sand.

The brigadier swung down and ran toward me, ducking under the rotors. As he approached he straightened up and smiled.

"I thought we were going to give you the signal," he said. "We saw the smoke and came as we were."

I nodded. "Things got a bit ahead of themselves." I pointed to Abbas's body. "That's him. Did you pick up his girlfriend in the Jeep?"

He approached the body and stood staring down at him. "One of the choppers went after her. She want get far. Who is she?"

"Anna Molyboha, secretary of the church and Abbas's willing, adoring slave. She has a quarter of a million dollars with her, and a lot of information you might be interested in." He looked over at me curiously. I shrugged. "Or at least your friends at the Office of Dyspeptic Imbibers of Scotch might be."

He smiled and I pointed to the Jeep. "I have a quarter of a million dollars in spoils of war, plus two cases full of details of his offshore accounts. Our friends from Asgard can look at them, but they are mine. I am taking them to my accountant in Vegas, on my way to Pinedale."

He nodded. "Will you be passing by New York?"

"I have an appointment there I have to keep."

"Will you be coming back?"

I sighed and looked up at the perfect blue sky, marred by the trailing smoke and the ugly smell of blood.

"I don't know, sir. Do me a favor, will you? Check his DNA, see if it matches the hand."

He looked surprised. "Why?"

"I don't know. A hunch."

His cell rang and he answered it, watching me.

"Yes," he listened for a moment, then, "What do you mean she disappeared?" He listened again, frowning at me, said, "Well keep searching. She has to be there! Get a chopper up to search from the air."

He hung up. "She's disappeared."

I nodded. "Call me and let me know about his hand, will you?"

———

MEANWHILE, over six thousand miles away, in a small office overlooking Mokhovaya Street in Moscow, Colonel Alexandrina Vitsin sat motionless at her desk. The city outside was dark and silent. Her face was expressionless, but deep creases cut down her cheeks to her thin, nicotine-stained lips. A cup of black coffee grew cold on her desk. Her telephone lay beside the cold coffee.

Its sudden jangling was startling in the silence. Her eyes flicked to the screen and she lifted it to her ear.

"Colonel Vitsin," she said. She listened in silence to the agitated female voice on the other end. Finally she said, "Be calm. You have money and you have American passport. Get a bus to Tijuana. Then go to San Diego. Book into hotel. Call me when you are there and I will bring you in for debriefing. What about Abbas?"

A thin, cruel smile touched her ugly lips. "Good," she said, and hung up.

———

IN PUERTO PEÑASCO ANNA hung up the telephone in the small bar and stepped out into the street. Above her she saw a military helicopter flying north and west toward Tijuana, and she wondered who was onboard, while nine hundred miles to the north and east, Dr. Claire Erickson in Pinedale, Wyoming picked up her telephone and smiled.

"My goodness," she said. "I am going to have to start believing you are serious. Did you finish your job?"

The voice on the other end said, "I hope so. I just have to stop over in New York and Vegas, and then I think I am coming home."

That made her smile.

Don't miss THE DEVIL'S VENGEANCE. The riveting sequel in the Harry Bauer Thriller series.

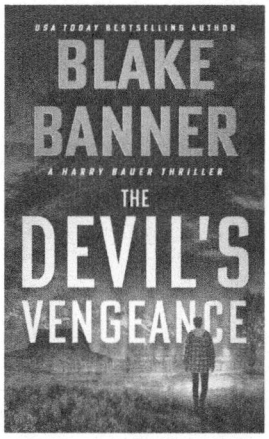

Scan the QR code below to purchase THE DEVIL'S VENGEANCE.

Or go to: righthouse.com/the-devils-vengeance

NOTE: flip to the very end to read an exclusive sneak peak...

DON'T MISS ANYTHING!

If you want to stay up to date on all new releases in this series, with this author, or with any of our new deals, you can do so by joining our newsletters below.

In addition, you will immediately gain access to our entire *Right House VIP Library*, which includes many riveting Mystery and Thriller novels for your enjoyment!

righthouse.com/email

(Easy to unsubscribe. No spam. Ever.)

ALSO BY BLAKE BANNER

Up to date books can be found at:
www.righthouse.com/blake-banner

ROGUE THRILLERS
Gates of Hell (Book 1)
Hell's Fury (Book 2)

ALEX MASON THRILLERS
Odin (Book 1)
Ice Cold Spy (Book 2)
Mason's Law (Book 3)
Assets and Liabilities (Book 4)
Russian Roulette (Book 5)
Executive Order (Book 6)
Dead Man Talking (Book 7)
All The King's Men (Book 8)
Flashpoint (Book 9)
Brotherhood of the Goat (Book 10)
Dead Hot (Book 11)
Blood on Megiddo (Book 12)
Son of Hell (Book 13)

HARRY BAUER THRILLER SERIES
Dead of Night (Book 1)
Dying Breath (Book 2)
The Einstaat Brief (Book 3)
Quantum Kill (Book 4)
Immortal Hate (Book 5)
The Silent Blade (Book 6)
LA: Wild Justice (Book 7)

ABOUT US

Right House is an independent publisher created by authors for readers. We specialize in Action, Thriller, Mystery, and Crime novels.

If you enjoyed this novel, then there is a good chance you will like what else we have to offer! Please stay up to date by using any of the links below.

Join our mailing lists to stay up to date --> righthouse.com/email
Visit our website --> righthouse.com
Contact us --> contact@righthouse.com

facebook.com/righthousebooks
x.com/righthousebooks
instagram.com/righthousebooks

EXCLUSIVE SNEAK PEAK OF...

THE DEVIL'S VENGEANCE

CHAPTER 1

THE ONLY SOUND WAS THE CREAKING OF THE SACK AS it swung, listless on its chains. The birds had been going crazy with their bedtime chatter, but as the sun had touched the tips of the Wind River Mountains over in the east they had gone quiet. I had stopped beating the sack and, sweating in the cool evening breeze, I had grabbed a towel and sat on the steps of my new house. The house that had belonged to Ash before he died.

I heard a footfall on the decking behind me and turned to look. Doc Claire Erickson was emerging from the house with two cold beers. She smiled, sat beside me and gave me a lingering kiss on the mouth. It was something I was having to get used to. It wasn't all that hard.

She linked her arm through mine and rested her head on my shoulder. It was a brief moment, but it was a moment of that feeling I had been searching for all my life. I smiled and touched her hair. After a moment of silence she said, "There is something I need to talk to you about."

I smiled down at her. "Is this that 'sit down we need to talk' conversation? We've only been living together for a month."

"No, of course not, I have never been happier, Harry." Then she tilted her head, sighed and shrugged. "Well, yes and no."

"Seriously?"

She straightened up. "Don't worry. It's nothing serious. It's just that, I've been offered a job. It's only for six months. I wouldn't even consider it, only," she turned to examine my face, "it's helping children and families who have suffered the consequences of recent war or civil conflict. There is so much of that these days, and there are so many children suffering."

I nodded and took a pull on my beer. "Where?"

"Burunda. I'd never even heard of it. It's between the Congo and Uganda."

I nodded again and looked down the long path where, not so long ago, I had watched Sheriff Seth Levi approach in his Jeep. I said:

"Is the organization called Better Tomorrows?"

She turned, surprised. "How on Earth did you know? Harry! Have you been reading my mail?"

I laughed. "Of course not. They wrote to me too. That's a very dangerous part of the world, Claire. Especially for attractive young female doctors. The president, George Majok, is known to be extremely corrupt and despotic. The crime rate is through the roof."

She looked away and straightened her back. "Don't patronize me, Harry."

"I am not patronizing you, Claire. It's a statistical fact."

Her cheeks flushed. "Oh, *your* job wasn't dangerous?"

I nodded, still gazing at the gate a quarter of a mile away. "Yup. Did you ask me to quit?"

She sighed. "Yes—"

"Did I quit?"

"Yes. You did. I'm sorry. But Harry, this is important to me. I have wanted to do something like this since college, and I have never had the chance. It is just six months—"

"You don't need my permission, Claire."

"I don't *want* your permission. But as a couple we need to agree on things like this. Otherwise what the hell are we doing together? What I *do* want, and I know it's a lot to ask, Harry, I want your blessing."

My jaw seemed to be cemented shut. I took a deep breath and tried to force something positive out of my mouth. But it wasn't happening. I shook my head, shrugged and spread my hands.

"My blessing? I'm not a priest or a holy man. The best I can do is my support and my backing."

She sighed. "What did they write to you about?"

"They wanted a donation, and they wanted to know if I would consider some kind of position on the board of trustees."

Her jaw dropped and her eyebrows shot up. "But, Harry, that's fantastic! You've always wanted to do something like that. When were you going to tell me?"

"Now, but you got there first."

She shifted her position so she was facing me and grabbed my hand in both of hers. "But, this is wonderful! We could go together! You could teach. You have so many skills you could share!"

"You have no idea how dangerous it is in that part of the world, Claire. I wish you'd—"

"Harry, it's a British protectorate. They have a governor and the British Army is out there, along with Oxfam, and apparently the crime rate is lower than the neighboring countries."

"Lower than South Sudan, Uganda and the Democratic Republic of the Congo is not much of a guarantee. We were going to get married, remember?"

"Of course I remember. And we can have a wonderful wedding when we get back."

"Wonderful, in the November snow. Will you do me a favor, Claire? Will you think about it for twenty-four hours? Islamic jihadists are very active down there. They come over the border from Sudan. For them murder and rape are routine, and if you're an American woman you are beneath contempt. If we go, you need to be fully aware of the risks we are taking."

"OK, I'll think about it. And if I still want to go tomorrow?"

"I'll make the donation and accept their offer on the condition I can accompany you wherever you're going on your six-month posting. But I want a promise from you. You told me you wanted me to give up my work because it was dangerous. What you want to do is at least as dangerous as what I did. So if we do this, that's it."

"I promise."

There was no "if" about it. She had made up her mind and I had known from the moment she mentioned it that she intended to go. And where I probably would not have accepted a post on the board of trustees, as it was I made a very handsome donation and made it clear it was conditional on my accompanying Claire wherever she was sent. They were understanding and accommodating, and within a couple of weeks Claire had her flight booked to Apodo-Djamu International Airport, in the Republic of Burunda.

I had wanted to travel with her, but I had stuff I wanted to attend to first in New York, and the board had wanted an urgent meeting with me before I departed. So I had booked a private long-range air taxi from Teterboro, in New Jersey, and arranged to meet with Luis Gabriel Camacho and Jean Fenlon, two of the senior trustees, at their offices on the sixteenth floor of an office block on 5th Avenue and East 69th, before my departure.

At Jackson Hole airport, as the early sun was turning the horizon blood red, I kissed Claire and saw her off at departures. She clung to me hard and whispered in my ear, "*Don't be long.*"

"I've chartered a Bombardier 800. It has actual beds and is almost supersonic," I told her. "I might even get there before you."

She laughed and started to cry, then thumped me on the chest a couple of times. "At the Imperial Victoria Hotel, on Independence Avenue. We have the Honeymoon Suite. You be there."

"You know it."

"You *will* be there."

"You know I will."

"I'm scared."

"I'll have a martini waiting for you in the bar, and a bottle of champagne in the room."

She gave me another kiss and hurried through security. I saw her turn and wave, and then she was gone. I felt a twist of nausea. The voice in my head told me I should have been firmer and stopped her from going. But I knew that would have been as good as holding a gun to our marriage and pulling the trigger, before we'd even walked up the aisle. At least this way I could be close to her and look out for her if anything happened.

Nothing would happen. I told myself that. Hundreds of people did this kind of thing every year and nothing happened. College kids did it to gain experience when they left university. It was no more dangerous than taking a walk in Soundview Park at dusk. I thought about that and didn't feel much better.

I had an air taxi booked for New Jersey and we probably took off before Claire did. The flight to Teterboro by private charter was slightly over three and a half hours, and we touched down at 11:30 AM. On the way I had looked into all the material I could get my hands on relating to Better Tomorrows. I don't trust charity organizations as a matter of principal. I think once you create an organization, you automatically create something that is more important than the people you're trying to help, and you also create the conditions for corruption.

And that's just the beginning. After that you start creating positions like CEOs, trustees, heads of department, directors and managers, and each post brings with it personal ambition, private interests and the urge for greater power. Each post is another nail in the coffin of your good intentions. But this gang didn't seem any worse than others I'd come across, and in any case, I was not in it for the charity. I was in it to protect Claire.

We touched down in a squeal of tortured tires and airbrakes, then taxied to a halt outside the terminal. The engines died and the door was opened by the stewardess. I gathered my things and climbed down from the plane to make my way through security. I

THE UNAVENGED | 175

had told Claire I was going to meet the trustees, and that was not a lie. I was. But before I met them, I had arranged to meet with the brigadier, and as I came through security I saw his Bentley parked outside. I crossed the lot and pulled open the front passenger door. He was behind the wheel, smiling at me.

"Harry, it's good to see you again. How's Claire?"

I climbed in beside him and pulled the door closed.

"It's one of the things I wanted to talk to you about. Right about now she's on her way to Apodo-Djamu, in Burunda. And she is about one tenth as scared as I am. So that makes her," I paused and nodded, looking out at the parking lot, "terrified."

It was typical of the brigadier that he made no comment, but simply fired up the big beast and pulled out onto Industrial Avenue. He turned right then toward Sylvan Avenue, the George Washington Bridge and Manhattan. It wasn't till we'd crossed the creek and were cruising up Route 9 toward the turnpike that he finally said, "What made her decide to go to Africa?"

"We're both going."

He glanced at me. "But you decided you wanted to have a chat with me first? What's this about, Harry?"

"I'm not sure. Maybe nothing. Better Tomorrows, a charitable organization that helps kids and families who are the victims of war. They reached out to Claire to do six months in Burunda, and at the same time they asked me for a donation and offered me a place on the board of trustees."

"Did that strike you as odd?"

I shrugged. "Not especially. I've been poking around some of the smaller charities. I've even set up a couple. I guess my name reached them."

He nodded. "So you decided you'd accept the offer so you could be with Claire and look after her."

"That's about the size of it."

He grunted. "Obviously you explained to her it's one of the most dangerous places on the planet right now. All its three borders are disputed, of course, though so far the disputes have been at a diplomatic level. But there is a significant Shiite population within Burunda who are quite active at the moment. It's a British protectorate, of course, and that gives it some stability. But our military presence is really quite small. We have more troops in South Sudan and Kenya than in Burunda.

"There is also a lot of violent crime, murder and rape. I'd say there is also a high potential for civil unrest that could spread across from South Sudan and Tubdhaawi in the north, on the border with Ethiopia." He was quiet for a moment, then asked, "Is that what you wanted, some intel on the situation out there?"

"Yeah, that's helpful. But I guess, when we last talked, we left things in the air. I guess I wanted to let you know that, when we come back from Burunda, I am going to retire. I'll work the ranch, I might even have kids and write my memoirs."

He nodded and smiled. "Good. We'll miss you, of course. I've known some good operatives, but you're among the best. And you know we'll always be here for you, if you should need any help."

"I appreciate it. Same goes."

"I thought lunch at Keens if you have time." I nodded. He went on, "Are you satisfied that Better Tomorrows is legit?"

"From what I have seen so far they seem to be above board. I have a meeting with two senior trustees later this afternoon."

"Good. I'll make some inquiries if you like, let you know what I find." We were moving down Broadway and turned onto West 36th. "You should have a think, Harry, before you swap your sword for a ploughshare, about who is left out there who would want to hurt you." He laughed suddenly as he pulled up a few yards from the restaurant. "Of course Jane would say that you had not left anyone alive who might want to hurt you!" The laughter faded from his face and he gently thumped the steering wheel with his palm. "But give it some thought. It's always a risk with us, when we retire."

He climbed out and I followed.

CHAPTER 2

LUNCH WAS BRIEF. WE DRANK WINE BY THE GLASS instead of by the bottle and had just one, small whiskey with coffee. We discussed the future, enemies who might want to get even with me, the political dynamics in central and northeastern Africa, and who I could call on if things got tough. He told me there were a couple of hundred British troops out there, at the Embassy and helping train the Burunda army.

"But the Regiment's not there." He held my eye. "If things go south, I'm afraid you'll be on your own."

BY THREE O'CLOCK I was climbing out of a cab on the corner of 5th Avenue and East 69th. The lobby was all shiny, toffee-colored marble, the elevator doors were beaten bronze and there were ferns and palms in urns big enough to live in.

On the 16th floor I stepped out directly into Better Tomorrows' lobby. I was the only passenger in the elevator and the only person in the lobby, besides the receptionist. I stood a moment looking around. The broad expanse of carpet was burnt sienna, the reception desk was a huge hunk of green marble, there were a couple of coffee tables discretely positioned behind large palms.

The walls were a pale beige but held huge canvasses depicting wild, impressionist jungle scenes in vibrant reds, yellows, blues and greens. The place stank of money.

The pretty girl behind reception was watching me and smiling. I smiled back and approached. She was wearing a sweatshirt with a picture of a cannabis leaf on it. It bore the legend, "Believe Nothing Till It's Officially Denied." She also had her hair in a ponytail and a ring in her nose that made me want to give her my handkerchief.

"Hi," she said, like she meant it.

"I have an appointment with Luis Camacho and Jean Fenlon. My name is—"

"Harry Bauer, they're expecting you, Mr. Bauer. If you'll give me one..." She didn't finish. She pressed a button and put a phone to her ear. "Hey, Jean, Mr. Bauer is here?" She made it sound like a question, then grinned. "OK, I'll tell—" She stopped and laughed harder, then showed me her teeth and told me, "She'll be with you right—oh! Here she is!"

I turned as a section of beige wall swung open and a woman emerged. She had crazy dark hair in what looked like a loose Afro, high cheekbones and startling, deep blue eyes. You couldn't describe her as anything but beautiful, and she had the kind of easy, spontaneous smile that made you want to be around her.

"Mr. Bauer, I'm Jean. It's good of you to come at such short notice, and I know you would much rather be with your wife." She took my hand and shook it with both of hers. "Please, won't you come through? Luis is anxious to meet you. We are really thrilled to have you onboard."

I followed her down a beige and dark wood corridor with concealed lighting, past appropriately ethnic pictures on the walls, and into a room at the end that was large and had panoramic views of 5th Avenue and Central Park. A long, oval table stood in the middle with a dozen chairs ranged around it. There was one guy sitting there. He stood up as I came in and smiled, extending his hand.

He wasn't what I had expected. With a name like Luis Camacho I had expected him to look Latino. But this guy was as tall as me, with blond hair, blue eyes and pale skin. He even had freckles. If you'd told me his name was Shamus McTavish I wouldn't have batted an eyelid.

He had strong hands and a good grip.

"Harry! I suppose we should be on first-name terms, right? Please, sit. Coffee? Tea? We are so pumped to have you with us." I opened my mouth to speak as I sat but he stopped me. "And your donation! Generous doesn't cover it. It will make such a difference to so many children and families."

I nodded. "I'm happy to help. Luis."

Jean spoke up. "There are just a couple of things, Harry. And please don't take this amiss, we have all had to go through this process because of the very delicate nature of our enterprise. Do you mind answering a couple of questions?"

I leaned back in my chair, frowning at her. "No, but I seem to remember you approached me, and you didn't have a problem accepting my donation. If you don't like my answers are you going to give me back the money?"

Jean became serious, but Luis threw back his head and laughed out loud.

"Harry! Harry! Please don't take offence. As Jean says, we have all had to answer these questions. There is no question of not liking the answers, but we do have to know who we have on the board, because we deal in such volatile situations. Our first and greatest concern is the children and their families."

I nodded, turned my attention to Jean and said, "Shoot."

She gave a tight smile. "You were in the British Army for a few years. Can you tell me about that?"

I shrugged. "There isn't much to tell. I was young, I came from a broken family. I don't remember my father. He disappeared when I was just two. My mother was an alcoholic and occasional drug abuser. So as soon as I had the chance I left home, left the country and joined the most bad-ass unit I could find.

That was the British Special Air Service. I was with them for eight years, and they are still like a family to me."

She nodded, then wet her lips with the tip of her tongue as she studied the surface of the table.

"You were not asked to leave, but neither did you receive an honorable discharge. You resigned. What's the story behind that?"

I narrowed my eyes and studied her a little more closely. "You do your homework."

"As I said, this is not personal, but we have to know whom we are dealing with."

"We were in Afghanistan. We had captured a man who was responsible for murdering and torturing the men, women and children of an entire village. The women and the female children were systematically raped before being killed. I, and the other guys in my unit, had to watch as this happened. When we caught this guy, the CIA turned up and wanted to take him away. I knew what that meant. It meant he had intel and skills they wanted and they were going to set him up in a safe house with a pension in exchange for the help he could provide them regarding the Taliban, Al-Qaeda and their relationship with Pakistan. I didn't think that was right."

"What happened?"

"I proposed that rather than let the bastard get away we should execute him there and then. The CIA senior officer complained to my senior officer and I was offered the opportunity of resigning and avoiding embarrassment for myself and the regiment. So that's what I did."

Luis leaned forward, with his elbows on the table. "Harry, in retrospect, do you regret having done what you did?"

"What I regret, Luis, is not having shot the bastard when I had the chance, before the CIA turned up. If that disqualifies me from being on your board of trustees—"

"Please." It was Jean. "Nobody is saying that, Harry. You can relax your defensive position. Please remember, we are all about the children. I think I can speak for Luis when I say that, if we had witnessed what you witnessed we would probably have felt the same."

Luis smiled. "My family is from Mexico, Harry. I lived there till I was five and I have returned often. I have brothers and sisters there. Nobody who has not seen those atrocities firsthand can have any idea what it is like. That is why we are here, that is why we have set up this charity. Every one of us has experienced something similar, and we want to make a difference."

I stared at him long and hard. "You're serious."

Jean said, "We're not here to judge, Harry. We're here for the kids. Is there anything else you feel you ought to share with us?"

I shook my head. "No."

She waited, watching me like she expected me to change my mind. When I didn't she said, "When you got back from the UK you were pretty broke. Do you mind telling us how you made your money?"

"Yes, I do mind. I worked freelance on a few classified projects and made a lot of money, which I invested wisely."

Luis said, "That's good enough for me."

Jean smiled at him and nodded. "Me too." Then she turned to me. "We just had those two question marks. Thank you for clearing them up. Now, we know that you were keen to accompany Dr. Erickson in Burunda, and we are delighted for you to do that. So, what we thought was that perhaps you could liaise with Chris Van Hurt and Adolfo Suarez, who are our administrative managers out there, and take charge of setting things up."

"Setting things up?"

"We will provide you with a file. It contains everything you could possibly need to know, from names and addresses to the overall goals and objectives of the organization in Burunda. Anything that's missing, you call us on the hotline. I suggest you read the outline on the way over and then take a few days to talk to Chris and Adolfo, study the file and then take it from there."

I thought about it and made a cautiously affirmative face.

"This would be during the six months that Claire is out there. After that I take her home and go back to breeding horses."

"That is absolutely understood. We are quite sure that a man like you can make a big difference in six months. After three months, if you still feel the same way, we'll send you somebody to groom."

We chatted for another ten minutes while an assistant went to get a large attaché case which proved to be full of all those documents she had mentioned, and included a couple of phone numbers where I could contact Chris Van Hurt and Adolfo Suarez.

After that it was a taxi back to Teterboro Airport, then a short wait while they finished fueling up the Bombardier Global 8000, one of the few private jets that could cover the seven thousand miles from New Jersey to Burunda nonstop. At a cruising speed of seven hundred miles per hour, it was still going to be a ten-hour flight, so I would have plenty of time to do my homework.

As it was I had a superficial look at the file, memorized a couple of names and numbers and noted the location of the organization's two field operations. They had their head office on Independence Avenue, and then they had Project One in the remote southwest of the country in the jungle just twenty miles from the border with the Democratic Republic of the Congo.

The other, Project Two, was in the northeast, roughly equidistant from the borders with Uganda and South Sudan—about fifteen miles from each. Only here instead of jungle it was more savannah, with small, gnarled trees and dry, red and yellow dust.

I had a couple of martinis while I read through the material. Then I had a sirloin steak and a shower and slept for four hours in the large bed provided in my suite.

By the time I had risen, showered and dressed, and was having coffee and hot buttered croissants, it was one AM in New York and in my body clock, but it was seven AM in Apodo-Djamu, the capital of Burunda.

The city, as I looked down on it through the window,

184 | BLAKE BANNER

consisted of a high-rise center clustered with tall towers of steel and glass, glinting dark gray and blue in the early sun, and then a sprawl of shantytowns stretching out like a vast spider's web in all directions. Those parts that were closest to the center were almost suburban, with houses made of brick, wood and thatch, with gardens and even swimming pools; but as they spread further from the city center, corrugated metal replaced roofing tiles, shacks replaced houses and the tropical gardens were replaced by patches of bare land with a few scattered cows and goats, bathed in the dim amber light of early morning.

Beyond that were the lean-tos, the collections of pallets and rags that were the closest some human beings ever got to home, where spirits were born strangled and died stunted and robbed of hope.

We skimmed over these fleeting images and moments later touched the tarmac at Apodo-Djamu International Airport in a scream of tortured tires and the surging roar of airbrakes. Then we slowed and taxied sedately to the VIP terminal.

I was clearly expected because the customs officials, who were all wearing khaki shorts, treated me like visiting royalty and waved me through, and told me my passport was, "quite unnecessary, Mr. Bauer!"

There weren't many other people at the airport, apart from men in khaki shorts all laughing and joking with each other like kids at their first dance. It was large, marble, echoing and empty and as I passed, virtually ignored, through passport control and into arrivals, in the echoing emptiness I saw a café with a single guy sitting at a table with a coffee, reading the paper.

He looked up as I approached him, smiled and stood, extending his hand. When he spoke he had that South African clipped rasp. "Mr. Bauer?" When I told him I was he gripped my hand like he wanted to strangle it and said, "Chris Van Hurt. It's an honor. Flight OK?"

He made *Chris* sound like *Cruss* and *it's* like *ut's*. I figured I'd get used to it.

"Flight was good," I told him, "but I'm keen to get to the hotel. I'm not sure if my fiancée has arrived yet. I'm keen to see her before anything else."

"Yuh, yuh I bet. Your bags are in the car. We can talk while we drive. The Imperial Victoria, right?"

We made our way out of the building and into the fresh morning. The sun had risen and was tinting everything with a bronze glow. There was a Bentley waiting and he gestured me toward it. As I climbed in the back I kept hearing him say, "...talk as we drive..." I watched him climb in beside me and asked him, "Has Claire arrived yet?"

"Yuh," he said again. "Yuh, she got here about six hours ago." He pulled the door closed. I gave a small laugh. "Damn. I was hoping to beat her to it and meet her with a martini."

The car pulled away from the sidewalk and we headed for the highway.

"That's something we need to discuss," he said.

I stared at him and the situation felt suddenly dangerous. "What, my meeting my fiancée with a martini is something we need to discuss?"

"No, your fiancée. We need to discuss Dr. Erickson."

My frown was turning into a scowl. "What do we need to discuss about her? And I suggest any discussing we do about her, we do in front of her."

"Well, that's just it," he said. "We can't, because it seems she's been abducted."

Scan the QR code below to purchase THE DEVIL'S VENGEANCE.
Or go to: righthouse.com/the-devils-vengeance

Made in United States
Orlando, FL
28 December 2025

75885010R00114